A Candlelight Ecstasy Romance ™

"YOU DRIVE ME CRAZY," HE GROANED. "GOD, I NEED YOU."

Somehow, Devon dragged herself back to reality. He had said he *needed* her, not that he loved her. At least that first time he had uttered the lie, making surrender irresistible. But this time she had to resist because love was what she wanted from him.

"No, Ryan, no," she whispered, tensing beneath him. "I . . . I can't."

"Yes, you can," he whispered back against her parted lips. "You need me, too. I know you do."

MORNING ALWAYS COMES

Donna Kimel Vitek

A CANDLELIGHT ECSTASY ROMANCE™

Published by
Dell Publishing Co., Inc.
1 Dag Hammarskjold Plaza
New York, New York 10017

Dell ® TM 681510, Dell Publishing Co., Inc.
Candlelight Ecstasy Romance™ is a trademark of
Dell Publishing Co., Inc., New York, New York.
ISBN: 0-440-16185-1
Printed in the United States of America
First printing—October 1982

To Our Readers:

We have been delighted with your enthusiastic response to Candlelight Ecstasy Romances™, and we thank you for the interest you have shown in this exciting series.

In the upcoming months we will continue to present the distinctive sensuous love stories you have come to expect only from Ecstasy. We look forward to bringing you many more books from your favorite authors and also the very finest work from new authors of contemporary romantic fiction.

As always, we are striving to present the unique, absorbing love stories that you enjoy most—books that are more than ordinary romance.

Your suggestions and comments are always welcome. Please write to us at the address below.

Sincerely,

The Editors
Candlelight Romances
1 Dag Hammarskjold Plaza
New York, New York 10017

CHAPTER ONE

Smiling up at the office supervisor, Devon Andrews pushed a wayward strand of silvery blond hair back from a porcelain-smooth cheek. "Really, it's tempting, but I usually just have a nice chef's salad at the grill across the street," she explained, her voice soft with a hint of an attractive lilt. "You know, just a light meal. Thanks for asking me to join you, though."

"Oh, come on," Isabel Hunt persisted, a determined gleam in her warm blue eyes. Thin hands perched on equally thin hips as she tapped her toe against the carpeted floor. "You've eaten a salad at that grill every day for the two weeks you've been working here, and I think it's time you join all of us who enjoy food that isn't really good for us. You'll be turning into a rabbit soon if you're not careful. And, Lord knows, you're slim enough to eat something more fattening than vegetables. Lucky girl."

"Look who's talking," Devon retorted with a grin. Her wide green eyes lost some of their usual dreamy luminosity and instead sparkled with amusement. "You're much slimmer than I am, Isabel."

"I'm just naturally tall and lanky," the supervisor insisted, eyeing Devon appraisingly. "You're what my mother always called nicely rounded—petite and squeezable, the kind of girl men can't resist."

After glancing down at herself automatically, Devon shrugged. "I'm not particularly interested in being squeezable or squeezed, thank you," she said wryly. "And I assure you I'll never be irresistible."

"Let's find out. We'll go eat something really fattening to start making you more squeezable than you already are. Now, come one."

A moment later, all her arguments squelched, Devon finally acquiesced. After tidying her desk, she hurried along with Isabel. They rode down in the elevator to the lobby, then out into the early May sunshine.

"Fabulous day, isn't it?" Isabel enthused, lifting her face to the sun-drenched blue sky. "I always feel so much more alive this time of year, don't you?"

"It is nice," Devon answered vaguely. Chewing her lower lip, she stared at the border of oaks enclosing the park across the street. All the trees and the flowering shrubs were burgeoning with new life once again. Yet the pale green leaves of the oaks and maples and the deep-rose-colored blossoms of the evergreen camellias aroused disturbing memories. She turned back to Isabel to escape them.

"Oh, I've been meaning to tell you that you have an admirer," the older woman announced abruptly with a teasing grin. "Remember a young man named Roger Dixon? In personnel? He met you the first day you came to work for us."

After searching her brain for a moment, Devon finally recalled the tall pleasant-faced young man who had sat behind a desk too small for his long legs. "The tall, thin fellow? Yes, I remember him. He was very nice."

"He thought you were very nice, too," Isabel declared, a matchmaking gleam in her eyes. "Just yesterday he asked me if I thought you'd have dinner with him some evening. Well, I tried to tell him the two of you would look like Mutt and Jeff together, but that didn't deter him in the least. He obviously seems to find you potentially squeezable just the way you are."

Shaking her head, Devon smiled indulgently. "Isabel, you're impossible."

The older woman shrugged jovially. "Well, how about it?"

"How about what?"

"Would you have dinner with Roger one night?"

"Oh, I don't know," Devon murmured. "He was very nice, and I liked him but . . . I don't really want to get involved with anyone at the moment."

"I don't think he meant to ask you to elope with him," Isabel commented wryly. "For now, he just wants to take you to dinner."

Devon laughed. "Of course, you're right but . . . but does he remember that I have Jonathan? I mean, most young men wouldn't want to become involved in any way with a girl who's responsible for a four-month-old baby."

"It doesn't seem to bother Roger, and I'm sure he remembers about Jonathan. After all, he helped you complete your employee insurance form, didn't he? And you must have listed Jonathan as a dependent?"

"Yes, I suppose you're right." Straightening her shoulders resolutely, Devon suddenly nodded. "All right. Maybe I will go out with him if he asks me."

"Good girl," Isabel responded. "You need to get out and socialize more often. Remember, all work and no play makes Jill a dull girl. And tired as hell." Coming to an abrupt halt in the middle of the sidewalk, she gestured in the direction of a small Italian restaurant called, not surprisingly, Antonio's. "How do you like Italian cooking? The lasagna here is really fabulous and chock full of calories."

"Sure, why not?" Devon agreed, managing to sound somewhat enthusiastic though she really didn't feel very hungry. Inside the candlelit restaurant a moment later, however, the tantalizing aromas wafting from the kitchen piqued her appetite a little. After she and Isabel gave a mustachioed waiter their order, she tried to relax against the cushioned back of their booth.

Sitting back also, Isabel lit a long, skinny cigarette, then offered one to Devon almost as an afterthought.

"No, thanks, I don't smoke often."

Isabel grimaced comically. "Would you believe I've tried to kick the habit eight times in the past two years? No will power, that's my trouble."

Devon disagreed. "I can't really buy that excuse, Isabel. You seem like a very strong-willed lady to me. Maybe you just don't want to stop smoking."

"Maybe not. Or maybe I just try to appear strong-willed so I can survive at home." Isabel chuckled affectionately. "You have to act that way when you have a husband and three children all demanding your attention. But I guess you know how demanding a child can be, don't you, honey? Then again, Jonathan is worth some sacrifices, isn't he? He's a real little doll."

"He *is* a beautiful child," Devon said softly, her delicate features relaxing in a loving smile, an animated sparkle suddenly illuminating her green eyes. "Did I tell you how active he's getting? He must move around in his crib all night. Every time I check on him, he's in a different spot. And when I hold him, he strains against my arms, trying to get a look at everything around."

"And he's only four months old! My, my, he's pretty young to be that rambunctious."

"Yes, but I think he's just naturally curious." Devon smiled indulgently. "Sometimes I think he's aching to run around and get his hands into everything he sees. And he's very strong. I believe he'll start crawling and walking very early."

"Must be unusually coordinated," Isabel commented. "Was his father the athletic type?"

Shifting uncomfortably in her seat, Devon clenched her hands together in her lap. "Yes, Jonathan's father was in good shape physically," she answered softly. "You know, the lean and muscular type, very active."

"I believe my oldest son, Jeff, is growing into that kind of man," Isabel said conversationally. "Even though he's only fourteen, he's as tall as an eighteen-year-old and very athletic. Lord knows where he got such coordination, though. It certainly didn't come from me, and Bill is sort of clumsy in a lovable way, if you know what I mean. So Jeff couldn't have inherited his prowess from him. Of course, my brother, Terry, is . . ."

As Isabel recited her family history, Devon was able to breathe normally again, relieved that Jonathan's father was no longer the topic of discussion. She hated to lie, yet was not quite to the point where she could confide in Isabel. Maybe later Devon could tell her the truth. Now it was simply too soon; she wasn't ready to confide in anyone. Luckily for her, their food was served a few minutes later, and Isabel began trying to coerce her into eating everything on her plate, keeping herself far too busy to ask any more personal questions.

"What's wrong with the lasagna?" she asked immediately when Devon folded her napkin and put it aside. "Why, you hardly ate anything."

"Oh, I did too. I ate nearly half of it," Devon protested laughingly. "Besides, that serving was generous enough for two people."

"Two very small people, maybe," Isabel scolded, then proceeded to intone a lengthy sermon on the merits of proper nutrition.

Since the only response needed was an occasional nod of her head, Devon settled herself comfortably on the padded seat and slowly sipped her red wine, allowing her gaze to wander to the other patrons in the restaurant. Her eyes lingered on a tall man near the bar who was talking to the headwaiter, but when he turned his head and she saw his face clearly, her breath suddenly caught in her throat. He looked like Ryan Wilder! For a frightening

second, everything before her went crazily out of focus, then she was overwhelmed by year-old memories.
. . .

Near the end of her first year as an assistant librarian at the university, she had met Ryan. A Texas cattle rancher and environmentalist, he had come to Boston to deliver a series of lectures on the necessity of protecting the world ecology. From his first day, Devon heard all the feminine whispers about him. When she finally caught a glimpse of him a day or so later, she could understand why all the women found him such a fascinating topic of conversation. Tall and slim, yet muscular, with finely chiseled bronze good looks, he seemed able to captivate every female who saw him. Yet in the beginning it was his voice that drew Devon to him.

She attended one of his lectures. Seated near the front, she rested her chin in one cupped hand and listened intently to his soft Texas drawl. His deep-timbred voice was melodious, almost sensuous somehow, and she could detect his abiding love for the land in every word he uttered. Yet his defense of the environment was less emotional than practical—cattle couldn't graze on polluted land, and after all, raising cattle was his business. His entire lecture was intriguing, even more so for Devon because his dark-blue eyes caught hers on several occasions. When she walked home alone later that evening, she remembered his soft, deep drawl and wry sense of humor and smiled.

Two days later, while Devon was alone in one of the offices of the library, Ryan strolled in, and she greeted him with a compliment on his lecture. He accepted the compliment easily, then asked her out to dinner. Though she was frankly surprised by the abrupt, unexpected invitation, she found herself accepting without hesitation.

All things considered, they should have had little in common. She was a city girl, fascinated by literature and delighted with her position at the library since it enabled her to make contacts in the publishing business. An aspiring writer of historical fiction, she knew she could use all the contacts she could cultivate. On the other hand, Ryan was a Texas rancher, well attuned to nature and protective of the land he loved so well. She was something of an idealist, while he possessed a more analytical mind. While he could completely solve Rubik's Cube in less than two minutes, she was lucky to arrange one side in that same amount of time. Yet, despite their different life-styles, Devon discovered to her delight that he was well-read, exceedingly intelligent, and that their feelings about important issues weren't so very dissimilar. It was only much later that she decided the old axiom must be true, opposites attract. In that budding May, however, she was far too intrigued with Ryan to realize that.

Their first evening together was enjoyable as they began to become acquainted. The night ended rather anticlimactically for Devon, however. Though their attraction to each other seemed almost tangible, Ryan didn't kiss her good-night. When he did kiss her during their third evening together, she was already half in love with him and totally unable to resist the compellingly intense passion conveyed by the demanding lips that parted hers. From that moment, their relationship deepened so swiftly and with such poignant urgency that the following days were a combination of heaven and hell. Ryan wanted her and since he had awakened in her an intense need to express her love for him, the inevitable happened. She spent a glorious night with him in his hotel suite, learning eagerly all he taught about the physical and emotional pleasures of lovemaking. Morning came, but brought Devon no regrets. After all, Ryan loved her too and had asked her to marry him.

All day at the library, Devon thought only of seeing Ryan again that evening, but he telephoned from the airport late in the afternoon, saying he had been called to Houston where his father was critically ill in the Texas

Medical Center. He would phone her the next day, and he would write. He promised.

He had never called. No letters had ever come. Finally, as the long weeks passed, Devon had been forced to accept the fact that all he had ever wanted from her was that one night. He hadn't loved her and he wouldn't be coming back. He had taken what she had offered so lovingly, then left her with a few bittersweet, dreamlike memories and an agonizingly real pregnancy. And the pregnancy was difficult. In the early months, she had felt so ill that she had had to miss work often and finally felt compelled to resign her position at the university library. She had been told that her job could not be held for her until she'd had her baby anyway. She could have opted for abortion, but she was never able to seriously consider it. Loving Ryan as she had, she already loved their child, and if her career aspirations had to be postponed for a while, she could accept that. Yet, she really had no idea what her immediate future held. Out of work, her savings dwindling, she couldn't imagine what she was going to do until her landlord, Ben Andrews, a retired English professor, realized her situation and offered marriage and legitimacy for her unborn child in exchange for her companionship. Ben was a kind man; she trusted him. And lacking any real alternative, she had married him. They had looked after each other until he had died over two months before her baby was born. After Jonathan came, she had realized how demanding a new baby could be. Needing a job less time-consuming than her position at the library had been, she had sought clerical work with the insurance company.
. . .

Now, sitting in the restaurant with Isabel, Devon tried to think only of how well she was beginning to rebuild her life. Yet, her stomach knotted painfully. She blinked her eyes several times, then wished she hadn't. The man by the bar still looked like Ryan, so much like him that she felt paralyzed by the conflicting emotions that began raging in

14

her. Then, as she stared involuntarily, the man's eyes met her own and something so much like recognition appeared on his lean face that a nauseating fear gripped her. Jerking her head around, she stared blindly at Isabel. "Oh, God," she whispered. "Oh, my God, it just can't be!"

Isabel clutched her arm. "What is it, honey? Are you feeling sick or something? What's the matter? Your face has gone white as a sheet!"

"Th . . . that man," Devon gasped, her eyes wide. "That tall man by the bar, look and see what he's doing, please."

"Why, he isn't doing much of anything, just looking this way," Isabel reported bewilderedly. "But wait, I guess you could really say he's staring over here. What's wrong, Devon? Do you know him?"

"He looks like . . . like . . ."

"Wait, he's coming over," Isabel interrupted in a whisper, eyeing the younger woman worriedly. "You do look like you're going to faint. Can't you try to take a deep breath?"

Obeying automatically, Devon felt some of her panic subside as a protective numbness spread throughout her body, making her limp and completely unable to return Isabel's reassuring smile.

"There now, you're looking a little better," the older woman whispered. "Take a little sip of your wine. He's almost here."

Devon hardly heard her. The blessed numbness deserted her too swiftly and her heart began to pound, thudding painfully against her breasts. Her mouth was dry, and when out of the corner of her eye she saw the man step to the table, she felt as if she were choking as her throat constricted.

"Hello, Devon," was all he said as she reluctantly lifted her head. She forced her eyes to meet the deep, dark blue of his for a fraction of a second before dropping them again to stare fixedly at the smooth brown column of his neck. It was no longer possible to deceive herself by saying

15

he couldn't be Ryan. He was. The seconds seemed to tick by with excruciating slowness. She was unable to speak for a moment until her pride suddenly took control. A forced smile thinned her lips for an instant, then was gone as quickly as it had appeared.

"Hello, Ryan," she managed to say with admirable calm. "What a surprise to see you here." Turning to Isabel, she made the necessary introductions.

Isabel stared up at Ryan, her expression confused and very curious. But she sounded quite natural as she said, "How do you do, Mr. Wilder."

"Mrs. Hunt," he responded politely, but he turned back to Devon immediately, his expression unreadable as his gaze drifted slowly over her. "You're thinner than you were the last time I saw you, aren't you? I hope you haven't been ill?"

"No, just dieting," she lied stiffly, clasping her hands together in her lap, trying to feel only furious contempt for him but having little luck. At the moment, all she could feel was a debilitating dread of the sleepless nights she knew would result from this meeting. She pushed that dread aside though. She could worry about insomnia later. Right now she had this moment to survive, and she meant to survive it with all her dignity intact. Resentment suddenly lifted her small chin and she met Ryan's enigmatic gaze directly again. "And you're thinner too. I suppose you've been working hard, rounding up cattle or whatever it is you do on those big Texas ranches."

"I don't spend my entire life in a saddle, Devon," he answered pointedly. "There's the business side to ranching too, though lately I've been prone to neglect it. Other . . . things on my mind, unfortunately."

"Oh," Devon muttered awkwardly. "That's a shame."

"Yes, a shame." Thrusting his hands deep into the pockets of his sand-colored trousers, he stared down at her rather broodingly, his jaw clenched, as he muttered

abruptly, "I have to talk to you. How about tonight? Are you busy?"

"I got married," she announced just as abruptly, hoping to shock him and feeling more than a little disappointed when her words elicited no visible reaction at all. His dark expression didn't alter and her shoulders drooped slightly as she looked up at him for a moment longer before averting her eyes. "You . . . you remember Benjamin Andrews? He owned those apartments where I lived. I married him."

Muttering incomprehensively, Ryan suddenly bent down over her, his palms pressed flat on the tabletop, his warm, minty breath stirring the wisp of hair that brushed her temple. "I still have to talk to you," he said roughly. "If not tonight, then now. I'm certain Mrs. Hunt would let me borrow you for a few minutes, wouldn't you, Mrs. Hunt?"

Isabel's startled expression was almost comical. "Well, I . . . I don't know. If Devon wants . . ."

"I can't talk, Ryan," Devon interrupted hastily. "I have to go now or I'll be late getting back to the office." She stood, willing her trembling legs to support her weight as Ryan moved closer to her, so close that his muscular thigh brushed against her own. She backed away, murmuring a quick good-bye, then took a sharp surprised breath as strong fingers closed urgently around her delicate wrist.

"Let me go, Ryan," she whispered furiously. "I don't want to talk to you and I have to get back to work. This is a new job and I want to keep it."

"But, Devon, for God's sake, I have to know why—"

Unable to endure his touch another minute, she wrenched her arm free and marched away, squaring her shoulders defensively as she threaded her way among the tables. She didn't slow her pace until Isabel caught her arm and guided her into the ladies' lounge.

"I think I'd better sit down," Devon muttered, sinking onto a chair, no longer able to maintain a show of bravado. Leaning her head back, she closed her eyes. "Oh, God, why did I have to see him now? I've been trying so hard to forget and now . . . now I'll have to start all over again." Swallowing convulsively, she pressed trembling fingers against her lips. "Oh, I don't feel very well."

"Don't move. I'll run in here and get a wet paper towel," Isabel said worriedly, scurrying away through the swinging door into the adjoining bathroom. In only a moment, she was back, folding the damp brown towel and laying it gently on Devon's forehead. She hovered by the chair, shaking her head and clicking her tongue against the back of her teeth. "Honey, you're so pale. You're positively white. I think I'll have somebody call a doctor. After all, you just had that baby four months ago and with the difficult labor you went through, maybe . . ."

"No, I'll be fine, really I will; just give me a minute to catch my breath," Devon said, opening her eyes again, trying to smile but not quite succeeding. As she sat up straight, she removed the towel from her forehead and stared down at the floor. "It's just a shock, running into him like this. I really never expected to see him again."

"Would you like to talk about it?" Isabel asked gently. "I'd be happy to listen if you think it might help make you feel better."

"I'm not sure where to begin. It's all so complicated. Lord, if only he hadn't decided to come back here again."

"Again? Then I presume you knew him here?"

Twirling a strand of her shoulder-length hair, Devon nodded. "We met when he was here last spring."

"And it's fairly obvious you weren't just casual acquaintances. I suppose you were in love with him, weren't you?"

A hint of a rueful smile tugged at the corners of Devon's mouth. "I guess saying I was in love with him is putting it too mildly."

"And what about him? Was he in love with you?"

"I thought he was, but . . ." Shredding the paper towel, Devon chuckled mirthlessly. "You wouldn't believe what

18

a gullible little simpleton I was a year ago. I was rather stupid, actually."

"Oh, surely not stupid. Maybe just young," Isabel said, attempting to give comfort. "You were only twenty-two last year. And this Wilder man, how old is he, anyway? Obviously much older than you."

"He was only thirty-four. That didn't seem so much older."

"A twelve-year difference is a pretty big one, honey, especially when a man is . . . well, like your Ryan Wilder. I can understand how you got involved with him, he's very attractive and he seems nice. And that voice . . ." Isabel sighed dramatically. "So don't blame yourself too much. Twenty-two is very young, maybe too young to be wise where love is concerned."

Devon shrugged. "Well, I'm a lot wiser now, and I sure feel much, much older than I did this time last year. Maybe it's true, wisdom does come with age."

Nodding, Isabel rummaged through her purse for cigarettes and a lighter, then halted her search abruptly, a small frown furrowing her brow. "I don't mean to be nosy, really," she murmured rather uncomfortably, "but you said you were involved with him last spring. But weren't you married then? I mean, since Jonathan's four months old, I just assumed . . ."

"I was pregnant when I married Ben," Devon confessed bluntly, unwilling to lie. "More than two months pregnant, actually."

"But how . . . Oh, I see. You were involved with both Ben and Ryan at the same time. Is that it?"

"No, not really. It was nothing like that at all," Devon said dully, deciding she might as well put an end to all Isabel's speculations. Drawing a deep breath, she gazed pensively at the tattered towel she held in her hands. "You see, I've never been sexually involved with any man *except* Ryan."

19

The older woman's eyes widened with sudden understanding. "Then . . . then that must mean . . ."

Nodding, Devon muttered, "That's exactly what it means—Ryan is Jonathan's father."

"Oh, my Lord, no wonder seeing him upset you so much!" Clicking her tongue against her teeth again, Isabel flopped down on the opposite chair. "Did he . . . Surely, he didn't just walk out on you when you became pregnant?"

"He didn't, no. I mean, he never knew I was pregnant. He couldn't have. I never saw him after . . . after that last night we spent together . . . He promised he'd be in touch with me, but of course I never heard a word from him."

"Then he still doesn't know about Jonathan, does he?" Isabel exclaimed, sitting up straight. "But why don't you tell him now? Don't you think you should? Maybe if he knew, he'd want to help you in some way, at least."

"I do have some pride," Devon said indignantly. "And I'd rather have nothing at all from Ryan than to know he was only helping me because he felt obligated to." She massaged her throbbing temples wearily. "No. I don't want anything from him that he feels he should give, not even money. Besides, I don't know what he might do if he found out about Jonathan. What if he wanted to become more involved in his life than I'd want him to? I mean, since he obviously didn't care about my feelings last year, why should I think he'd care about them now?"

"But still, he's the child's father. He has a right to know about him, doesn't he?" Isabel suggested very gently. "Don't you really think he does?"

"No, I *don't!*" Devon retorted vehemently. "After what he did, he has no rights at all. And I'll never give him another chance to turn my world upside down again. I've started a new life now and Ryan Wilder's not going to mess it up for me. I won't let him. I plan to just forget I even saw him this afternoon."

Yet even as she lifted her chin in a show of bravado, her

own words echoed in her mind, hollow and meaningless. There simply are some moments in life beyond forgetting. For Devon, seeing Ryan was one of those moments, and deep in her heart she knew it.

CHAPTER TWO

"You don't have to answer this if you don't want to but
. . . but I guess you were never really married then, were
you?" Isabel asked as she and Devon walked back to the
building where they worked. "Did you just decide it would
be simpler to tell people you're a widow?"

"Oh, no. All that's true. I did marry Benjamin Andrews
and he did die." Devon shrugged. "Of course, I did let
people assume the marriage was perfectly normal and that
Ben was Jonathan's father. That *did* seem simpler than
trying to explain about Ryan or trying to make anybody
understand that Ben and I had more of an arrangement
than a marriage."

"An arrangement? What kind of arrangement?"

"A very simple one: I needed a place to stay and a name
for my baby. And Ben needed somebody to be with him.
He knew he was dying and since he had no relatives and
no close friends, he was willing to marry me just to have
someone around who cared about what happened to him.
I think he was terrified of the prospect of dying all alone."

Isabel shook her head sadly. "Oh, honey, wasn't that
terribly depressing for you?"

Shrugging again, Devon sighed. "Sometimes it was, but
Ben was very philosophical about his illness. His wife had
been dead three years and he still missed her very much.
He said there wasn't much to live for without her, anyway.
Actually, he married me mostly because he said I remind-
ed him of the way his wife had looked years ago. So

naturally he was very good to me. He treated me like a daughter really. I was only depressed when he'd start talking about Ryan."

"He knew Ryan? How?"

"Well, he didn't *know* him exactly. When Ryan and I were going out every evening, he'd pick me up at my apartment. Ben owned the apartments and lived down the hall from me, so naturally he'd seen Ryan. He never liked him, so he said. He thought Ryan was too old for me and far too experienced. Ben said he'd been afraid I'd end up hurt if I fell in love with him. He had been proven right, of course, but I didn't much want to hear that right then."

"Well, of course, you didn't," Isabel murmured sympathetically, giving Devon's arm a quick, comforting squeeze. "But tell me why you married Ben in the first place. Wasn't there something else you could do? What about your family? Wouldn't any of them help you?"

"There's only my great-aunt Ruth. She raised me after my parents were killed when I was ten. But she's a very straitlaced old lady. When I moved here into my own apartment, she told me I was asking for trouble and if I got myself into a mess, I might as well not ask her to help me get out of it." Devon smiled ruefully. "Well, I did get desperate enough when I realized I was pregnant to call her anyway and ask if I could come home. She said no, that I'd made my bed, and so on. So that only left Ben. Actually, I was much better off with him. He was much nicer to me than she would have been."

Isabel smiled understandingly. "And he only wanted companionship from you? Nothing else?"

"He wasn't interested in me sexually, if that's what you mean," Devon said emphatically. "Oh, no, I never would have married him if he'd wanted . . . wanted that kind of relationship. And he never tried to . . . He never tried anything."

"That made it easier for you then. You had enough

23

problems as it was. That way, he was like a father, wasn't he? And at least you didn't have to worry about money."

"No, and he left me a little in his will besides setting up a small trust fund for the baby."

"He must have been very fond of you to leave you provided for. That apartment house alone is great security for you."

"But he sold that right before we got married. He was really too ill to worry about managing it, and since I was pregnant, he wouldn't hear of me trying to handle it. He thought it would be too tiring for me. And he needed the cash to pay his medical bills, anyway. But he was very good to me. I don't know what I would have done if he hadn't been. I just hope I made his last days a little less lonely."

"I'm sure you did, honey."

A brief silence followed as they entered the office building and headed to the bank of elevators. But Devon sensed that Isabel had more she wanted to say. "All right, what do you have on your mind?" she asked abruptly, smiling at the older woman's sudden sheepish expression as they stepped into the waiting elevator.

"Well, it's . . . Now, I hope you won't take this wrong, but don't you think maybe you should talk to Ryan about . . . about Jonathan?"

"No, I don't," Devon reiterated almost irritably as they stepped off the elevator at the seventh floor. "I don't want to talk to him about anything. I can look after my son and myself just fine. I don't want Ryan's charity."

"You loved him very much, didn't you? Are you sure you aren't afraid you still do?" Isabel probed gently. "If that's true, you can't escape it by refusing to see him. You'd be better off facing him."

"I don't happen to think so," Devon said stiffly. "And I can't imagine what he wants to say to me anyway. It's a little too late for talk."

"Maybe he would be able to explain what happened,"

Isabel suggested hopefully. "Maybe there was some reason he couldn't write to you."

"Goodness, I didn't know you were such a romantic," Devon retorted wryly, not realizing her eyes mirrored the unhappiness she was trying so desperately to conceal. "But I'm afraid no excuse Ryan could give would ever be good enough to make me forgive him."

"Are you sure of that? He looked like he could be a very persuasive young man to me," Isabel said innocently, then walked across the huge room to the cubicle that was her office.

Watching her go, Devon removed the soft plastic cover from her typewriter and took a deep, shaky breath. She inserted a sheet of paper in the typewriter, determined to concentrate only on making her fingers hit the correct keys, nothing else.

That evening, after feeding Jonathan, Devon tucked him into bed for his afterdinner nap. Standing beside his crib, she patted his well-padded bottom gently until his eyes flickered shut. A weary sigh escaped her as she gazed down at him. He was so much like his father. Seeing Ryan today had merely served to re-emphasize the resemblance. Jonathan had the same thick dark-brown hair and the same blue eyes that could cloud to gray when something displeased him. What would Ryan think of his son? she wondered wistfully, then shook her head in disgust, pushing that futile question aside.

Tiptoeing out of the nursery, Devon looked around the nicely furnished living room. Ben had moved her into this apartment a week before their wedding. It had pleased him very much to provide such a nice place for her to live. Yet, it was too nice. Ben had paid the rent for two years in advance, but when that time was up Devon knew she would have to move. She'd never be able to pay the exorbitant rent on her salary. Extras like the swimming pool and tennis court exclusively for tenants' use made it far too expensive for her to remain. But she was certain she and Jonathan could be quite content in more modest surroundings. It was the moving itself that she dreaded.

"I'll worry about that later," she said aloud. Twirling a strand of hair, she went into the small but cheery kitchen, made a sandwich, then sat down at the table to eat. Her appetite was nonexistent though, and she had to force each bite past the constriction in her throat that had been there since seeing Ryan. She needed to cry but refused to. A year ago she had done so much crying, and she had found that giving in to her battered emotions accomplished almost nothing. The pain still remained after the tears had ceased. Only occasionally had she been able to cry herself into an exhausted sleep. Most of the nights had been spent lying awake, tortured by thoughts of Ryan. Remembering the bone weariness that had plagued her then and feeling that lethargy beginning to sweep over her again, Devon thrust aside her plate, her sandwich only half-eaten. Grim determination tightened her lips. She would not endure more than one night without sleep this time, not with a nearly full bottle of sleeping pills sitting on a shelf in the bathroom medicine chest. Tonight she would try to sleep without taking one of the pills, but if she tossed and turned for hours, tomorrow night would be different. After all, her doctor had said getting plenty of rest was essential if she wanted to go on working every day and caring for Jonathan at night. That's why he'd prescribed the pills.

Pushing back her chair, she got up to tidy the kitchen, then walked into her bedroom again. A relaxing bath was what she needed; it would be best to take it now while Jonathan was still napping. From a drawer in the bureau beside her bed, she took a freshly laundered pair of faded denim jeans and a white cotton-knit top, then went into the bathroom to fill the tub with soothingly warm water.

After a thirty-minute soak, Devon felt some of her tension easing. She dressed and brushed her hair until it lay on her shoulders like a silken curtain flashing with silver light and then stood before the mirror, gently pinching some color into her pale cheeks.

Satisfied she no longer looked as weary as she had an hour ago, she wandered into the living room, glancing at the alarm clock by the bed. It was only twenty till seven, too early for Jonathan to wake up yet. She settled herself on the brown easy chair to pass the time until the baby did awake and opened the novel she had been reading, tucking her bare feet up beside her. Unfortunately, she could not concentrate, and finally, after finding herself hopelessly lost in the plot, she closed the book with a sigh. She squeezed her eyes shut, trying to eradicate the image of Ryan's face, but the effort was useless. All she could think of was the piercing blue eyes that had stared almost challengingly at her today and the fascinating beating pulse she had noticed in his temple as he had bent over the table, his face close to hers. She had detected the familiar, clean, masculine fragrance of his aftershave, a scent that had evoked a host of nearly unbearable memories, which she had suppressed all afternoon. But she couldn't suppress them now. Suddenly she was recalling the taut smoothness of his brown skin and the corded muscles of the shoulders she had caressed. With a soft moan, she relived that first taking thrust of his hard body, which had been accompanied by whispered endearments and a gentle, coaxing parting of her lips by his until the fleeting pain had been overwhelmed by the ecstasy of finally belonging to him.

But he had obviously not wanted her to belong to him, and his leaving should have killed all her desire, she reminded herself bleakly, trying to purge all the burning memories from her tired brain. That was not so easy. He had looked too good to her today; she had been torn apart by the need to escape him and an equally strong need for him to touch her.

"Idiot," she called herself. When someone suddenly

27

knocked at her door, relief washed over her. Any distraction was welcome at the moment.

"Who is it?" she called softly as she approached the door. When only silence answered her question, she frowned slightly and repeated, "Who is it, please?"

"It's Ryan. Open the door, Devon," that unmistakable voice commanded.

For one horrifying moment, she felt her heart stop beating. Then it began to thud wildly, and she looked around the room in desperation, as if seeking some avenue of escape. Her legs refused to move and trembled weakly as she clenched her hands together and bit back the little cry that was rising in her throat. Her entire body shook violently as Ryan spoke again.

"Damn it, Devon, let me in. I mean to talk to you, so you might as well open the door or I'll break it down, I promise you."

Recognizing the grim determination in his voice despite the soft low tone, Devon staggered over to unfasten the chain. After twisting the key, she turned the knob slowly, releasing the catch, then moved back quickly as Ryan swung the door open. Stepping inside, he pushed the door shut behind him, his narrowed eyes making a fast survey of the room before settling on Devon. He said nothing; he simply stared at her.

Devon returned his stare speechlessly until the silence between them became unbearable. "Wh . . . what do you want? Why have you come here?" she asked, her voice choked. Twisting her hands together, she started to turn away. "I wish you'd just go. We have nothing to say to each other."

"The hell we don't!" he muttered, catching her arm to jerk her back around to face him. "We have plenty to say, or at least I have plenty of questions for you to answer. And I'm not leaving until we've settled this."

"Until we've settled what? What is there to settle?" she asked with forced belligerence. He was too close. So close that she could feel the warmth emanating from his body. Lost only a moment ago in the erotic memories of his lovemaking, she could not react indifferently to him now. Clad in tight-fitting gray trousers and a black turtleneck sweater, he was so excitingly male. As his gaze seemed to linger disturbingly on her mouth, she felt a stirring inside her, a stirring that a year ago had always preceded a flaming of overwhelming needs. Hating herself, she tried to wrench her arm free, but his fingers dug into her flesh. At last her struggles ceased, and she cried impotently, "How did you find me here?"

"It was easy. Your dear husband's name is in the phone directory," Ryan muttered, glancing around the room. "And speaking of your husband, where is he?"

"He's . . . he's not here."

"What?" Ryan's smile was mocking as his eyes flicked over her slender body. "You mean he had something more important to do than to stay here with you? Foolish fellow. Now, if I were your husband, I'd take you to bed every evening after dinner, or better yet, before."

Devon gasped, her face paling. "I guess I should have expected you to say something that crude," she said, her voice strained, nearly breaking on the last word. She glared up at him. "I think you'd better just leave; I can't imagine why you came here in the first place."

"Can't you? Then I'll be happy to tell you." Something like fury glittered in Ryan's icy, blue eyes. "I just wanted to see what a handsome couple you and Ben make—you looking like you're about sixteen and him old enough to be your grandfather."

"Well, since he's not here, you wasted your time coming, didn't you?" she snapped back. "Sorry."

"No need to be," Ryan said with infuriating calm as he released her arm, then strode to the sofa and sat down. Stretching his long legs out in front of him, he settled back. "I'll just wait until your loving hubby returns."

As the strength suddenly drained from her legs, Devon sank down on the edge of a straight-backed wooden chair.

"Why are you doing this?" she asked indignantly. "What exactly do you want?"

"Why did you marry Andrews?" he answered with a question, his voice hard and relentless. "You never seemed all that fond of him when you and I were seeing each other. But I suppose his money began to appeal to you, didn't it? And you decided trading your body for his cash was a fairly good bargain. Isn't that right?"

"You . . . you . . . oh, God, you're despicable!" she gasped, fury making her reckless. "You shouldn't judge everybody by your own standards. I . . . I didn't marry Ben for his money, and he didn't marry me for . . . for . . ."

"Why did you marry then?" Ryan asked sarcastically. "Did the two of you just fall madly in love?"

"That's none of your business."

"But I think it is." With one fluid movement, Ryan straightened and leaned toward her, resting his elbows on his knees as he added, "You were a virgin until I made love to you, Devon. What I need to understand is how you left my bed and went straight to Andrews's. Was it his money? Or maybe his contacts with publishers appealed to you?"

Hadn't she endured enough without this, she thought, looking at the cruel expression on his face through resentful eyes. Why had he come here to torment her? She longed to throw the truth at him, to see his reaction when he heard another man had been kind enough to marry her when he had left her pregnant with his baby. What would his reaction be? Indifference? Or would telling him about his son only create more problems for her? Unwilling to take that risk, she could only scowl at him. "Just go away, Ryan," she commanded icily. "Just leave me alone."

Getting to his feet, he thrust his hands into his pockets and began to pace back and forth in front of her.

"No, I won't leave you alone," he announced abruptly, stopping to stare down at her. "At least I won't until you tell me why you never answered my letters."

For a moment Devon was too astounded to speak, then she shook her head disbelievingly.

"Letters? How could I answer letters you never sent, letters you never even thought about writing?" she asked incredulously. "What's the point of all this, Ryan? Why even pretend you wrote to me now?"

"My God, you're amazing! I'm pretending nothing and you damn well know it!"

Jumping up, she clenched her fists at her sides.

"You never wrote! Not a single word. I waited and waited for a letter to come and finally I realized you'd forgotten all about me!"

"Forgotten?" he muttered, shaking his head and smiling unpleasantly. "Look, I don't know what kind of game you're playing right now, but I can tell you I'm not buying a word of this sad little story you're handing me. I know you got my letters."

"And I know you never wrote any!"

With a harsh sigh of disgust, he raked his fingers through his dark hair. "And I suppose you're going to try to tell me I didn't call you twice either? And that I didn't fly up here to see why you hadn't written me?"

"What kind of nonsense are you trying to hand me?" she snapped at him. "Of course, you never . . ."

"You know I did, Devon," he interrupted, actually managing to sound bitter. "With my father on his deathbed, I left him and flew here to see why you hadn't bothered to answer even one letter of mine in six weeks, but you weren't here. Andrews informed me that you'd taken off for New York for a meeting with one of your precious publishing contacts. With Dad so sick, I couldn't wait for you to get back here, but I told Andrews to have you call me. But you never did. You're not a very reliable message answerer, are you, Devon?"

31

He was the one who was amazing, she thought, her entire body shaking violently. He must think she was the greatest fool in the world, and she certainly would be if she believed the outrageous lies he had just uttered. "I never got any *messages,*" she retorted at last. "How could I when you never called to leave any? And surely you can't expect me to really believe you ever came back here to see me? I would have known if you had because I certainly wasn't in New York then. I . . . if I recall correctly, I . . . wasn't feeling very well then, and I was probably in bed in my apartment when you *say* you came. So why didn't I see you? You never came knocking on my door, and you know it."

"No need. Andrews met me outside and told me about your New York trip." With a sudden chilling laugh, Ryan sat down again. "But why don't we just let him settle this little disagreement. Have you forgotten he took my messages?" Smiling unpleasantly, he took a plain silver case from his pocket and extracted a cigarette. As he lit it, he gazed at her over the lighter's orange flame. "It should be interesting when old Ben comes home, don't you think? He can hardly lie to my face and say he never saw me. I imagine he'll be as mystified as I am about your denial. So when do you expect him back? Do you think I could have a drink while I wait for him?"

Twisting her hands nervously, Devon glanced over at the clock, appalled when she saw it was already seven twenty. Jonathan usually awakened about this time, and before he did and started crying to be picked up, she had to get Ryan out of the apartment. "Ryan, all this is so useless. Why don't you just go," she said, her tone more pleading than she had meant it to be.

"What's the matter?" he taunted. "Afraid old Ben will find out what a little liar you can be?"

"Oh, for God's sake, Ben can't find out anything!" she blurted out. "He died months ago."

"You're lying again," Ryan muttered, his eyes taking on a dangerous glitter. "Aren't you, Devon?"

"Would you care to see the death certificate?" she asked mockingly, glancing at the closed door to Jonathan's room again. "He *is* dead, Ryan, so there's no point in carrying out your bluff any longer. I *know* you never wrote or called or came. I don't need Ben to confirm that for me. So if you've had enough fun at my expense, I want you to get out of here."

Ryan hardly seemed to hear her. A different kind of light now gleamed in his eyes as they moved with deliberate slowness over her tensed body. "If Ben's dead, then that means you're—" His words halted abruptly. He jerked his head around toward Jonathan's door as the child began to cry, seeking rescue from his crib. Ryan's eyes darted back to Devon's paling face. "A baby? You have a baby?"

Paralyzed by dread, she could only stare at him, her eyes wide. She couldn't breathe until Ryan got up and started toward the closed door. Then her breath was expelled in a rasping gasp of dismay. "No, you can't go in there! He . . . he's afraid of strangers."

"But I can't leave without seeing your baby, can I, Devon?" Ryan replied, grasping her shoulders and moving her aside when she tried to stop him. Brushing off the small fingers that clutched at his arm, he opened the door.

Devon heard his sharp intake of breath and knowing what it might mean, searched her brain frantically for some convincing lie to tell him.

"How old is this baby?" Ryan finally asked, his voice hard as he turned back to her. The expression on his lean face was grim, almost dangerous. "How old, Devon?"

"Six weeks," she lied, then gasped again as he shook his head and reached out to roughly grab her by the shoulders.

"I don't happen to be totally ignorant about babies," he informed her mockingly. "The wife of our ranch foreman has had three of them in the past five years and not one of them was as big at six weeks as this child. So how old is he really?"

"Jonathan is just 1 . . . large for his age." Half frantic, she struggled to free herself from his fierce grip, but to no avail. "Really, some children are just bigger than others."

"Not this much bigger!" he muttered harshly. "Now, you'd better tell me the truth or I'll shake it out of you, no matter how frail and delicate you look to me."

"Oh, for pity's sake," she exclaimed nervously. "Why in the world should you even care how old he is?"

Suddenly Ryan's grip on her tightened painfully, biting into her smooth, creamy flesh. He shook his head grimly, his eyes losing none of that debilitating piercing iciness. "He's my son, isn't he?" he practically growled. "Isn't he mine, Devon? I think he has to be. He's at least three months old."

"All right, all right! *Damn* you! He's almost four months old," she flung at him recklessly. "And, yes, he is your baby, I'm sorry to say!"

The lean contours of Ryan's face hardened until he actually looked capable of violence. "You had my child and didn't have the decency to tell me he existed," he ground out harshly. "What right did you think you had to keep his birth a secret from me?"

"I had every right! And you didn't and still don't have any," she cried, twisting to wrench free of him. When he refused to release her, she ceased struggling to stand stiffly before him. "Let me go, and move. I want to pick up *my* baby."

Though Ryan dropped his hands, he still blocked the way. Shaking his head, he wouldn't allow her to move past him. "Now I'm really confused," he admitted, his voice suddenly as low and gentle as she had remembered it to be. "Here you were, pregnant with my child, yet you still never contacted me. Why didn't you ever even answer my letters or my messages?"

"Oh, Ryan, you know damn well there were no messages to answer," she protested bitterly. "Why do you want to believe there were? Do you think you can convince me that I simply didn't get *any* of them? Well, you're wasting your time, I'm not quite that dumb."

"Let's not get into that argument again. It looks like a stalemate anyway. I'm certainly not going to say I didn't try to contact you, and you're obviously not going to admit that I did."

"But you didn't—" She was silenced by the brief touch of his fingers against her lips and the unyielding command in his voice.

"Enough," he proclaimed. "Maybe we'll settle that argument later, but for now we need to discuss what we're going to do about this situation."

Devon's heart lurched suddenly. What had that meant? Afraid to find out, she stepped forward, praying that this time he'd let her pass. "I . . . I'd better pick up Jonathan before he gets tired of waiting and starts howling again." When Ryan moved aside, she rushed past him to smile wanly down at the baby. "Hi there, sweetheart. Did you think I'd forgotten you?"

Jonathan's answer was a bubbly toothless smile and an enthusiastic waving of his arms. When she lifted him up against her shoulder, he clutched bunches of her T-shirt in his small, strong fists and leaned back against her supporting hand to get a better look around. Then his wandering gaze found Ryan and he was still, staring at his father curiously.

Devon's breath caught in her throat at the expression that was gentling Ryan's features. Whatever he felt about the baby was not indifference, and she groaned inwardly. Her worst fears were being realized—Ryan probably would not be willing to walk away now and forget his son existed. And if he wanted to become involved in Jonathan's life, that would mean he would also be involved in hers, a painful prospect. Foolish as it was, she still felt something for him, and even if it was only a physical attraction, that could be dangerous enough.

During the following two hours, Devon watched with an oppressive, ever-increasing dread as Ryan and Jonathan became acquainted. By nine thirty it was a great relief to gain her son's complete attention again by taking him into the kitchen to feed him. Yet even then, Ryan joined them, laughing softly as Jonathan's mouth opened eagerly for every spoonful of warm oatmeal and pureed fruit offered to him.

"He's a greedy little beggar, isn't he? Did you see the little glow that came into his eyes with that first spoonful of applesauce?"

"He likes to eat," Devon responded. Smiling rather wistfully, she looked up at Ryan, completely unaware of the aura of vulnerability conveyed by her dark-green eyes and the fragile contours of her small face.

He reached out to touch light fingertips to the delicate hollows in her cheeks. "God, Devon, you look tired," he whispered. "And there's something in your eyes that—"

"I'm fine," she interrupted, unwilling to accept even a little tenderness from him. Drawing back to escape the fingers on her cheeks, she wiped Jonathan's face with a damp cloth, smiling lovingly as his mouth opened eagerly again. "No, that's not your bottle, but it's coming. Just be patient until we get to the living room."

A moment later, she sat on the sofa, cradling the baby in her arms as he attacked the nipple of his bottle as if he had never before had anything to eat. Sensing Ryan watching her, she looked up reluctantly.

"I . . . I'm surprised you didn't choose to . . . to nurse him," he said with uncharacteristic hesitancy. "I mean, you just seem like a young woman who would see the rewards in breast-feeding. I'm not criticizing, I assure you, but . . ."

"I did nurse him, Ryan," she answered with a slight, understanding smile. "I'd still be nursing him now but

36

about two weeks ago he started getting impatient. He couldn't breastfeed and look around at the same time. He's so curious and I can keep the bottle in his mouth no matter how often he turns his head."

With a nod, Ryan leaned forward, a sudden determined frown creasing his brow. "I want to take care of my son and you, Devon," he announced quietly. "I don't want you to have to worry about anything except raising Jonathan. It'll be so much easier if I provide for—"

"Maybe it would be easier in some ways," she interjected tensely, defensive pride shimmering in her emerald eyes. "But we'll be perfectly all right without your money. Though I appreciate your offer, I don't want you to feel obligated in any way."

"Damn it, I don't feel obligated! I want to take care of both of you and I don't mean by just providing money. I want to be more to my son than just a man who sends a check every month, and I *intend* to be more than that." Ryan hesitated a moment, simply looking at her, then continued. "Actually, I think maybe we should even get married."

"Married!" Far too aware of the pain caused by his offhand suggestion, Devon masked her true feelings by resorting to sarcasm. "What a romantic proposal, but I'm going to have to say no to it. Marrying for the sake of a child would be a terrible mistake. There should be much more than that between a man and a woman."

Ryan cursed beneath his breath. "There was a great deal more than that a year ago, Devon. What happened to it?"

Chewing her lower lip, she shrugged. "Suppose you tell me what happened."

"How the devil should I know?" Some indefinable emotion flickered in his eyes, then died away in their cold graying. Resting his forearms on his knees, he clenched his hands together. A muscle ticked in his jaw. "But no matter what did happen, you'd better get something straight

37

—you've had my son and now that I know he exists, I don't plan to just forget him."

Bitter resentment washed over her. Angry spots of color flared in her cheeks. "Don't you think you'd better discuss this little situation with your fiancée? Her name's Iris, I believe. Why don't you go call dear Iris and see what she thinks of your newfound sense of paternal responsibility."

"Don't be ridiculous. You know my so-called engagement to Iris was strictly for my father's benefit. My father was dying. I felt the least I could do was humor him with a fake engagement." As Ryan finished, a sudden smug smile etched attractive creases into his cheeks beside his mouth. "Oh, Devon, you've slipped up, my dear. How could you have possibly known about Iris unless you *did* get my letter explaining the whole situation?"

At that moment, Devon felt she easily could have killed him. At the very least, she longed to slap that smile off his face. "I really can't believe you," she uttered stiffly over Jonathan's head. "You know very well I never heard about Iris from you. Oh, no, Ben showed me a Dallas paper one day about a month after you left here, and I *read* a society item that mentioned you and your *fiancée,* Iris Jenkins, one of Texas's foremost equestriennes. How convenient for you, her father's ranch bordering your own. Think of the money you'll save on fences someday. It was a pleasant surprise, I must say."

"I have to hand it to you," he retorted with a brusque laugh that did nothing to soften his ruthless expression. "You have an answer for everything." When Devon simply stared at him with impotent anger, he sat back again. "Since *our* son's fallen asleep, why don't you put him to bed before we settle this little disagreement."

Muttering beneath her breath, she did as he suggested, but only because her arms ached from holding the baby so long, she tried to tell herself. After tucking Jonathan into his crib, she tried to steady her frazzled nerves. Then she stepped back into the living room and frowned when

38

she found Ryan relaxing in his chair. His legs were out-stretched before him, as if he meant to stay awhile.

"Don't get too comfortable," she said tightly, hands on her hips. "This disagreement will never be settled so—"

"But it has to be; it will be. Jonathan's my son, too, Devon. I'm not going to just walk away from him."

Taking a deep breath, she felt her anger dissolve into a weariness of the spirit. She hadn't been prepared for a confrontation like this. She didn't want to argue with Ryan; she didn't even want to see him or think about him. She simply wanted him to go away and stop harassing her and told him that.

"But I'm not going away without Jonathan," he de-clared without hesitation. "My son's not going to have a life like I had, torn between my parents. My first fourteen years spent in New York with my mother, rarely seeing my Dad. And when she thought I was old enough to go stay with him on the ranch, he was practically a stranger to me. I don't want Jonathan to ever feel like I'm a strang-er. I *will* be a part of his life, starting now."

Devon's hands dropped limply as a tremulous sigh es-caped her. "I understand what you're saying. But, Jona-than . . . well, maybe he'd be better off without just a part-time father, and I . . . I want you to know I can survive very well without your charity."

Ryan sprang to his feet with pantherlike ease and was across the room in an instant, spanning her slender waist with strong, lean hands. "I'm not offering charity," he said, his tone adamant, his dark eyes gleaming with a strange light. "Pity is one emotion you've never evoked in me. So, for God's sake, stop being so obstinate. I want to help you and Jonathan, so let me. That's the only sensible answer."

"But will Iris think it's so sensible?" Devon asked sharply, desperate to ignore the needs his hands on her were arousing. "I don't really think she will, do you?"

"So that's what this is all about, isn't it? You never

wrote me or returned my calls because you got all in a huff about Iris? You didn't think I should do that for my father even though he was dying?"

"And how do I know he was ever even sick? I imagine he's made a miraculous recovery by now?"

"He's dead, Devon," Ryan said bluntly. "He clung to life for several months but . . ."

"Oh, damn, I'm sorry. I really am," she whispered, thoroughly ashamed of herself. Her eyes suddenly shimmered with tears for Ryan and for his father and for herself. "Why are we tearing each other apart this way? Let's just say good-bye and be done with it."

He shook his head emphatically. "No. There'll be no good-byes. I'm not losing my son now."

"But . . ."

His fingers dug into her waist. "Dammit, Devon, enough. You aren't going to keep me away from Jonathan. I'll make you very sorry if you even try to."

"But you can't just run across me in a restaurant, then decide to take over my life!"

"Little idiot, do you really think I just happened to run into you? Oh, no, I came to Boston specifically to see you." When she sniffed disbelievingly, his icy eyes held hers captive. "Of course, I didn't know I'd discover I had a son."

"I don't really care why you came here. All I care about is Jonathan. I'm his mother and I say whether or not you can see him," she exclaimed defiantly. "That's my right and mine alone and you'd be wise to remember that little fact." Stumbling back a step when he abruptly released her, she watched as he strode to the door and flung it open. When he turned quickly and looked back, she could only stare mutely at him.

"I have some rights in this matter, too, Devon, and I fully intend to exercise them," he announced coldly, relentlessly. "So *you'd* be wise to resign yourself to this fact—I will be back. Count on it."

As he closed the door on his way out, Devon walked woodenly to the sofa and sat down. After an anguished moment, she buried her face in her hands, unable to suppress her tears of frustration a second longer.

CHAPTER THREE

Ryan's threat hung over Devon like a cloud during the following days. Though common sense told her he could never force her to marry him, a nagging fear dragged constantly at her stomach. She spent every minute of every evening at home in a state of nervous agitation, waiting for the knock on the door. It was nearly impossible to eat and sleep never came easily. Even the happiness she had always found in Jonathan was diminished because of Ryan's visit. Now she could not look at her son without wondering if Ryan had been right in saying a child needed two parents to have a truly secure life. Yet, wouldn't it be better for her to try to provide that security alone than to marry a man who only felt obligated to care for her and their son? Of course, it would be better, she told herself repeatedly. It had to be. She had loved Ryan but he had left her, and now she was too proud to accept his charity. So he would simply have to forget about trying to create normalcy in a situation that was far from normal. He could even go back to his Iris with a clear conscience. It could hardly be his fault that Devon had refused his offer to help. If only she could force him to accept that refusal.

. . .

Although Devon knew Ryan could not make her do anything she didn't want to do, she feared that fact would not stop him from trying. After that Monday night, she had fully expected to see him the very next evening. But Tuesday had passed without a word from him. And

"Maybe it's not uncommon if there's some proof the mother is unfit to raise the child. But I am not an unfit mother!"

Frowning questioningly, Mr. Bradford glanced at Ryan, then cleared his throat again nervously as he received a slight nod from his client.

"There would . . . there *could* be ways to make the court doubt your fitness. Half-truths are sometimes very effective in damaging character, Mrs. Andrews. For example, Mr. Wilder could tell the court in all honesty that you married a man many years your senior, a man with property, a man who died only a few months after marrying you. I imagine you can recognize the veiled insinuation in such a statement."

"But you wouldn't!" Devon gasped disbelievingly. "You wouldn't try to insinuate that I . . . I had anything to do with Ben's death! You couldn't."

"No. *I* couldn't," Steven Bradford conceded gently. "I don't practice law that way, and if Mr. Wilder wished to employ such unethical tactics, I would naturally withdraw from the case. But I think you know he could easily find another attorney who would have no problem with the question of his professional integrity, and that kind of attorney would not care what sort of insinuation he would have to make about you—as long as he thought he could win for Mr. Wilder."

Turning her head toward Ryan, her eyes wide with shock, she desperately searched his face for some sign of compassion. "You wouldn't really do that to me, would you?" she whispered. "You couldn't?" When he only lifted his brows noncommittally, she felt as if he had slapped her. Her skin went cold and clammy and her cheeks blanched to a deathly white as she stammered, "B . . . but I have a lawyer too and . . . and he could prove those insinuations were totally false. Then you'd never win custody. You couldn't."

"Are you willing to take that chance, Devon?" Ryan

asked softly. "Ben didn't leave you enough money outside of that trust fund to hire a really expensive lawyer. I must say you don't look like you would be physically capable of withstanding a long, tense court battle. Of course, you can easily put an end to this unpleasantness before it begins by simply agreeing to marry me. Maybe you better take a few minutes to reconsider my proposal."

"Why don't I leave you two to discuss this alone?" Steven Bradford said rather eagerly, hastily shoving the papers he held into his briefcase. As he stood, he smiled weakly at Devon, his expression sympathetic and regretful. "I'm sorry we had to meet under these circumstances, Mrs. Andrews, and I hope you and Mr. Wilder can reach some agreement in this matter without taking it to court. I've been involved in many custody cases and they are usually painful for everyone concerned." He turned to Ryan. "Call me. Let me know what's decided."

Too stunned even to escort Bradford to the door, Devon merely watched silently as Ryan performed the courtesy for her. When he closed the door after the lawyer made a hasty exit, she looked away quickly, trying to hide the sudden tears that blurred her vision. Biting her lower lip, she willed the tears not to spill out onto her cheeks, but her will was not strong enough to suppress them. Several huge tears cascaded over her cheekbones, shimmering like crystal in the lamplight. Suddenly Ryan was bending over her, resting a hand on each arm of her chair.

"Devon, you made me do this," he said roughly, sighing as she shrank away from him. "What other choice did you give me? You refused to marry me. You gave me every indication that you would refuse any offer of help I made. And I got the distinct impression that you would discourage any effort I made to develop a close relationship with my son. What else could I do except see a lawyer?"

"All right, you win," she muttered, her eyes closed as she rested her head against the back of the chair. "I'll take

48

support money from you, and whenever you're in Boston you can visit Jonathan. Now are you satisfied?"

"Hardly," he replied, straightening to thrust his hands deep into the pockets of his navy-blue trousers. When her eyes flew open, he smiled mockingly. "Your offer isn't nearly good enough, Devon. In fact, I still think maybe we should get married."

"But why?" She jumped to her feet to stand stiff and defiant before him. Slapping back a strand of hair from her cheek, she stared up at him. "What possible good would it do for us to get married?"

"Someday it will probably mean something to Jonathan, don't you think?"

"Oh, Ryan, don't you dare try to use that baby to blackmail me!" Half turning away, Devon expelled her breath in an exasperated sigh. "Okay, I suppose it might mean something to Jonathan someday to know we were married, but . . . but what good will it do any of us now? We'll be here in Boston and you'll be a thousand miles away in Texas."

"Oh, good God, Devon, you can't mean you believe I plan to go off and leave you and Jonathan here? Oh, no. We'll get married here, then both of you will go home with me."

"You mean to Texas!" she cried incredulously, spinning back around on one heel. "You must be kidding! And when you've decided we've been married long enough to satisfy convention and we divorce, what am I supposed to do? Just come back to Boston and start all over, trying to make a future for Jonathan and myself?"

"We'll worry about the future later. Right now, it's the present we're concerned with."

"Well, that's easy for you to say, isn't it? You won't be the one who has to come back and start over!"

Ryan's hands shot out to grip her upper arms roughly. "Surely you don't imagine I'm going to walk away from my son when I've just learned of his existence?" he asked furiously, his eyes a glittering blue. "Don't you think you were selfish enough when you chose not to even write and tell me you were pregnant. You seem to forget that baby is just as much mine as he is yours. And if you won't marry me, I have only two choices. You force me to sue for custody or you willingly sign an affidavit verifying I am Jonathan's father *and,* both you and he will go back to Texas with me so I can see him whenever I want."

A great aching void engulfed Devon, overwhelming her defensive anger. Her life seemed to be careening rapidly out of her control. She couldn't let him coerce her into going with him. She simply couldn't. Nothing would be left of her pride if she had to live in the same house with him, seeing him every day, knowing he only tolerated her presence because he wanted his son with him. And she would know no one in Texas. She would be a stranger in a strange place, a thousand miles away from home, with little chance of finding anybody she could relate to. And Iris would be there, the woman Ryan obviously planned to marry. It tore Devon apart even to think of seeing them together. Oh, no, she couldn't face that prospect. She felt as if she had experienced enough pain to last a lifetime without adding that. Avoiding Ryan's watchful eyes, she shook her head. "I can't go to Texas. My doctor said I'm not strong enough yet to withstand a hot climate. He told me to avoid excessive heat at all costs," she exaggerated. "And since Texas is so dreadfully hot in the summer . . ."

"We actually do have air-conditioning in the boondocks, Devon. We don't exactly live in a sod house on the ranch," Ryan informed her flatly. "And, besides, even Boston can be sweltering, as you well know."

Devon's shoulders sagged. He defeated her at all turns. All she could do now was reason with him and hope he would be sensible. "Ryan, this is crazy. You don't want me there. And certainly Iris won't. Maybe we . . . could even get married if that's what you think we should do, but Jonathan and I will stay here. Any time you want to visit, you can. I'd even let you have Jonathan to yourself for a week or so, if you'd like that. But you just can't expect me to go to a place where I won't know anybody— I'd go crazy with loneliness."

"Devon, I'll be there," he whispered. With something akin to tenderness, he drew her close against him. "You won't be lonely."

She held herself stiffly in the circle of his arms, feeling only humiliation and an aching emptiness as he brushed his lips against her forehead. Pity was the last thing in the world she wanted from him.

"No, I won't go. I just won't."

With a gentle hand, he brushed back a strand of hair from her cheek, his fingers lingering. "My God, Devon, I just want to look after you. Why can't you let me?"

"I don't need you to look after me, that's why. I can look after myself just fine."

"You think you're very tough, don't you?" he asked softly, shaking his head. "Well, I don't think you are. I think you need a man in your life, as most women do."

Staring up at him in amazement, she retorted, "You sound like the worst kind of male chauvinist—"

"Now, now, now, no name calling," he interrupted with a grin.

"Oh, go to hell," she muttered, twisting free of the arms that gently imprisoned her. Sinking down on the sofa, she picked up the pack of cigarettes she had bought on impulse that afternoon, hoping smoking might ease some of her tension. Her eyes widened. The pack was empty. She had smoked all those cigarettes in one afternoon. Little wonder she felt rather queasy. Appalled at what she had done, she crushed the pack in her hand with a muffled exclamation of frustration.

"Here, have one of mine," Ryan offered, opening the silver cigarette case. "I didn't know you smoked though."

Refusing to admit that she usually didn't, she accepted

51

the cigarette he lit for her, then collapsed back on the sofa. "I won't go with you, Ryan," she announced abruptly in one last show of defiance. "I simply won't go. I don't want to be anywhere near you."

"Don't you?" He breathed harshly, moving so quickly that she had no time to react. Suddenly he was beside her on the sofa, one large hand encircling her slender neck while the other curved over her left hipbone, holding her fast. His mouth descended roughly on hers, parting her lips by force. The cigarette still in her hand, she couldn't do much to deter him. Then the warm possessiveness of his kiss began to make her want to press close to him. With a cry, she pushed hard at his chest with her free hand. His hold on her merely tightened. He hauled her forward until she was half-reclining across his muscular thighs. Then his touch lost all roughness. His hands caressed her, moving with nearly unbearable gentleness down her spine to the small of her back. His kiss became soft as a light breeze, brushing slowly back over her lips, deliberately tormenting.

An unbidden thrill shattered Devon's will to resist. *She wanted him.* Wanted him to kiss her with overpowering urgency again. A tremor of desire shook her, and with a tortured sigh the opening flower of her mouth sought his.

"All the old feeling isn't gone, is it, Devon?" he murmured huskily before his lips took complete possession of hers again.

When he took the cigarette from her to crush it out in the ashtray on the table beside him, Devon's hands involuntarily feathered over his shoulders, sliding up to cup his face. The kiss swiftly intensified and his teeth caught the full curve of her lower lip to tug her mouth open wide. The touch of the tip of his tongue against the tender veined flesh of her inner cheek evoked a soft gasp of exquisite pleasure. Her arms went around his neck, small fingers tangling in the thick, dark hair at his nape. She lay close to him, the enticing contours of her lithe body yielding softly to his superior strength.

Ryan touched her face, sensitive, featherlike fingertips tracing the delicate cheekbones, the arch of her brows, and the smooth line of her jaw. His hands dropped, his palms cupping the warm swell of the sides of her breast. With a muffled exclamation, he sought bare skin, easing his hands up beneath her shirt. Deftly, expertly, he unfastened the front closure of her bra to close his strong fingers over the satiny, cushioned softness that surged to fullness with his touch. He gently squeezed, explored the aroused rose-tipped peaks with slow, teasing strokes.

Devon trembled, swept away in the marauding power of the lips that plundered hers. Her entire being throbbed with the memory of that night when kisses like these had been a mere prelude to a satisfaction more joyfully intense than she had ever imagined. Aching for that joy again, she pressed closer to Ryan, her thighs brushing his side as she responded ardently to his masterful kiss. The sudden hardening of his lips was echoed throughout the length of his lean body.

It was only as he sought the button on the waistband of her jeans, when his fingers brushed evocatively over the bare skin of her abdomen, that she came to her senses. No man had touched her so intimately in over a year, and although Ryan was the man who had touched her then, she was jolted back to reality by his caresses which were too knowing, too evocative, too potentially devastating.

"Stop!" she gasped, fear overwhelming passion. With an earnest mutter of protest, she managed to escape the fierce onslaught of his mouth. "No, never again!"

"Never, Devon?" he queried, his whisper hoarse and powerfully seductive, his breathing labored. "But you do still want to be near me, don't you? Just the way you wanted to be near me last year. Remember?"

"No, and I don't want to remember!" she exclaimed, wrenching free to move away from him. "Can't you leave me alone? I'm not going to marry you and I'm not going to Texas! You can't expect me to do that. What about my friends here? My career . . ."

"Damn your career! You can write in Texas." Ryan's eyes bored into hers. "Or you can stay here if you please. But you'll stay alone because I'll take Jonathan home with me."

"You'll never be able to do that!"

"It could happen, Devon. Are you really prepared for a nasty custody battle?"

"But you wouldn't do . . ."

"Wouldn't I?" he retorted, rising to his feet. "But I will, I promise you that. I'll fight you for my son if you force me to."

At his ruthless tone, she gazed up at him, devastated by the latent power of his lean masculinity. He was so much stronger than she was, both physically and emotionally. In that moment, she was afraid she could not possibly win any battle with him. She sighed tremulously, blinking back the tears that rushed to her eyes. "All right, all right," she said so softly he could hardly hear. "I can't . . . won't marry you, but . . . but I'll go to Texas for a while. So now you've won. Since you've gotten everything you wanted, will you just get out of here and leave me alone."

"Fine," he said, his tone much lighter now and conveying obvious relief. "But I'll be back tomorrow. We'll make plans to leave in a day or two."

Unable even to lift her head, Devon heard only his departure. So many thoughts and emotions were bombarding her all at once that she felt dazed. She sat staring blindly into space, only stirring several minutes later when someone knocked on the door.

"Damn," she muttered tearfully, dragging herself to her feet. "What kind of trouble will this be?" When she reluctantly pulled open the door, her heart seemed to leap up into her throat at the sight of Ryan, leaning nonchalantly against the doorjamb. What now?

With a seemingly genuine smile, he straightened and handed her an unopened pack of cigarettes. "I thought you might want these." Before Devon could compose herself sufficiently to utter her thanks, he added too commandingly, "Just be sure you don't smoke them too quickly. They're the last cigarettes you're going to have for quite some time. You shouldn't smoke, you're too thin already."

Infuriated by his superior tone, Devon felt her cheeks burn fiercely. Uttering a very uncomplimentary curse beneath her breath, she thrust the cigarette pack back into his sun-bronzed hand and slammed the door on his still-smiling face.

CHAPTER FOUR

Looking out on the sparkling waters of the Gulf of Mexico, Corpus Christi, Texas, was pretty much like any other large city with tall, modern buildings, tempting, cool parks, and busy, broad streets. Devon sat beside Ryan in the taxi from the airport, holding a fretting Jonathan on her lap. The only appreciative difference she could see in this city was the profusion of dusky-pink oleander, which seemed to bloom everywhere. She was almost too tired to notice even that much. The flight from Boston had seemed endless and a Houston stopover had only served to prolong it. Glancing at Ryan, Devon noticed that even he looked somewhat weary, and she could not help wondering if he was thinking about Iris.

Suppressing a sigh, Devon closed her eyes and rested her head against the back of the seat. The past week had been hectic. Although her earthly possessions didn't amount to much, it had taken some time to pack everything for shipment. Rushed as she had been, she hadn't given even one day's notice to the company, and Isabel had informed her that the personnel director had not been at all pleased that she had quit so abruptly. In other words, her job would not be waiting for her should she ever want it back. Ironically, Isabel had also added that she thought it wildly romantic of Ryan to whisk Devon away to Texas, though Devon repeatedly told her that romance had nothing to do with it. Ryan only wanted his son. Devon could understand that, but she couldn't understand why he insisted on dragging them down to his ranch when it had to be perfectly obvious to anyone with good sense that his precious Iris would be far from happy with that arrangement.

Actually, Devon felt she didn't know what made Ryan do anything he did. Now, as the taxi slowed to a stop at a traffic signal, she peeked surreptitiously at the smooth, strong line of his jaw. Her arms tightened around Jonathan. It did not seem possible that she and this man who sat beside her had ever been close enough to create the child she held. How had she been able to give herself completely to him that night they had spent together? What about him had made her trust him without question? If only she knew, then perhaps she could prevent herself from ever trusting him again. But accomplishing that feat wouldn't be easy. She was still as physically attracted to him as she had ever been, and when he was not provoking her to anger, he was able to arouse frightening longings in her. There was no middle ground in her reactions to him. Either she felt like flailing her fists at him or flinging herself into his arms. And his reactions to her seemed to be similarly confusing. Sometimes he glared at her as if he longed to do her some bodily harm, but at other times his gaze became provocatively warm and lazy as it drifted slowly over her body, making her wonder if he was mentally undressing her. All in all, the situation Devon now found herself in seemed fraught with danger.

As she sat reminding herself to be cautious, Ryan turned his head, smiling a nearly irresistible slow, gentle smile at her. Her breath caught. It had been a long time since she'd seen him smile like that.

"You're very tired, aren't you?" he asked softly. "Would you like to rest your head against my shoulder?"

Though she would have liked it very much, she shook her head. "I better not. You might never be able to wake me up if I go to sleep now."

"Let me hold Jonathan then."

As Ryan's hands slipped beneath the sleeping baby, his knuckle grazed Devon's breast. She stiffened, feeling as if fire had touched bare skin, and as he lifted Jonathan off her lap, her eyes were drawn to the firm, sensuous curve of his lips. She forced herself to look away. What was wrong with her? she asked herself disgustedly. Surely her need for him to touch her had gotten her into enough trouble last year. She should have enough sense not to go skipping blithely down that path again. She simply had to control her emotions. She *would* control them. Lifting her chin resolutely, she turned her head to stare out the window.

A few minutes later, the taxi driver turned into the circular drive of a large hotel, pulling to a stop before a long, narrow canopy that covered the walk to the entrance. As a uniformed doorman rushed out to greet them, Devon turned back to Ryan, the expression on her face confused and questioning.

"I thought we'd stay in town a couple of nights before going on," he explained before she had a chance to ask why they were there. Something like tender indulgence gentled his features as his gaze drifted slowly over her and down at their son. "Both of you are very tired, I know. So I thought we might stop here and take a rest."

"Oh," she murmured, hoping he could not read her mind. The thought of spending the night in a hotel with him was far more disturbing than it should have been. But maybe she was just overly tired, she hoped as she stepped out of the taxi, then reached back inside to take Jonathan.

A minute later, as Ryan checked them in at the desk, Devon stood behind him, gazing out across the plush lobby. She *was* overly tired, she tried to reassure herself. Weariness from the long flight had simply allowed her mind to take a fanciful turn. After a good night's sleep, she would be able to react to Ryan more rationally. After all, he was no longer interested in her sexually, so she had no reason to fear that he might expect to share her bed tonight, or any other night, for that matter.

Sighing with impatience at her own adolescent imagination, she turned, listening to Ryan's deep, melodious voice as he talked to the desk clerk.

"I hope you have a suite vacant, Johnson," he was saying. "This time a single room won't do."

"Your stepmother must be with you this trip," the clerk said in a friendly tone. "It'll be good seeing her again. It's been a long time."

"Actually, Maggie isn't with me," Ryan said. "I'm here with my . . . uh, fiancée."

"Well, you don't say! Congratulations, Mr. Wilder." The clerk laughed knowingly. "I guess I shouldn't be surprised you finally decided to marry Miss Jenkins. When she was coming here to see you last time you stayed, I noticed she turned into some beautiful woman. She has about the prettiest chestnut hair I've ever seen. . . ."

Devon tried not to listen as the clerk droned on and on about the incomparable charms of Miss Jenkins, but with every word he uttered her limbs grew wearier. At last, Ryan corrected the man's mistake.

"I'm not engaged to Iris Jenkins, Johnson." Turning, he grasped Devon's elbow and drew her forward. "This is my fiancée, Devon, and our son, Jonathan."

The clerk's mouth nearly dropped open. If Devon had not been so exhausted, she might have found his reaction amusing. But as he looked Jonathan and her over speculatively and as what seemed to be a gleam of understanding lit his eyes, she felt more like crying than laughing. She met the man's stare steadily, however, knowing she'd be wise to become accustomed to being curiously inspected.

At last Ryan finished his business at the desk, and as a bellman gathered up their luggage, he took Jonathan again, cradling him easily in one arm. Cupping Devon's elbow in his free hand, he guided her to ornate wrought-iron doors of the elevator.

"I think you'll like staying here," he said as they exited the elevator on the seventh floor a minute later. "The service is excellent and it's a quiet place. You should be able to relax."

Though Devon doubted that, she did not have the energy to say so. With the careless remarks of the desk clerk, the little strength she had still possessed after the long flight had seemed to drain from her. All she wanted now was to crawl into bed and sleep. It wouldn't be that simple, though, because Jonathan would have to be given his dinner and his ten o'clock feeding before she could put him in bed for the night. Ah, well, she would undoubtedly survive, she decided as she preceded Ryan into their suite.

The sitting room was magnificent, decorated elegantly with simply designed mahogany furniture and carpeted with thick and springy cream-colored plush. Vibrantly hued oil paintings highlighted the walls, and Devon wondered if Ryan always indulged in such luxurious accommodations when he came into the city. Had he stayed in this very suite when Iris Jenkins came visiting last year? No, he couldn't have. He had told the desk clerk a single room wouldn't do this time. Even so, Devon thought it was rather tacky of him to bring her to the very hotel where he and Iris had conducted their little trysts. He should have been considerate enough to take Jonathan and her someplace where they wouldn't have had to endure speculative glances from curious clerks like Johnson.

"What should I do with Jonathan, Devon?" Ryan asked, interrupting her resentful thoughts as the bellman left the suite. Still cradling the baby in one arm, he gestured toward the door to the right. "They'll be putting the crib in there in a minute. After they've finished, shall I put him to bed?"

After dropping her purse on the blue brocade sofa, Devon went across the room to gaze indecisively at her son, smiling as his half-closed eyes widened at the sight of her, then began slowly to close again. As she squeezed his chubby little hand, she shook her head.

"No, I'd rather feed him before I put him down for his nap. Since he's half awake, let's try to keep him that way until we can get some food up here for him." Glancing around, she noticed for the first time that one of the walls was covered with mirror panels. "Let's put him down on the floor over there. I imagine he'll wake up when he catches sight of himself in the mirror. His pediatrician had a mirror beside his examining table and Jonathan loved to lie there and watch himself wiggle."

After she spread the quilted comforter, Ryan put the baby down. Then he straightened, laughing as Jonathan immediately turned his head toward his image and began to wave his arms and kick his legs energetically.

"You're a tricky little mother, aren't you?" Ryan asked teasingly as he turned to Devon who stood beside him. His smile faded and he reached out suddenly to lift a strand of hair back over her shoulder. His fingers lingered in the silky thickness as he murmured, "How did you feel when you realized you were pregnant with my baby?"

"Scared," she answered honestly. And lonely, she wanted to add, but didn't, fearing such an admission would be too revealing. Instead, she took a step backward, away from the disruptive touch of his fingers, shrugging as she avoided his eyes. "I was just scared. For a while that's all I felt."

"Scared of what?" he muttered curtly. "Scared Ben Andrews would realize it wasn't his child you were carrying?"

"Of course not! Ben knew it was your baby! I never tried to hide that fact from him. You just don't understand, do you, what a trauma an unexpected pregnancy can be? Suddenly, your whole world changes. I spent one night with you and before I knew it, there I was, responsible for another life. Let me tell you, that's enough to scare anybody! But, of course, men don't have to worry about such things, do they?"

"Oh, I worried, Devon," he said grimly, his mouth twisting self-derisively. "You wouldn't believe how many sleepless nights I spent, hating myself for what I'd done to you."

"I just bet you did," she retorted sarcastically. "And even if you had, wouldn't it have been a little too late to start worrying about the loss of my virginity?"

"Yes, obviously it was too late, but how the hell was I to know you'd use the loss of your virginity as an excuse to sell yourself to some old man with a little money and a few friends who could help your career?"

Devon's reaction to his mockery was instantaneous and uncontrollable. A dizzying desire for some sort of revenge swept over her and her hand shot up to deliver a stinging, hard slap to his tanned cheek.

For a moment there was only ominous silence in the room. Then, as a muscle began to jerk in Ryan's clenched jaw, he reached out swiftly to encircle her neck with one strong hand. "Sometimes I think I would enjoy snapping that fragile little neck of yours." Suddenly his thumb pressed hard against the throbbing pulse in her throat.

"Why bother?" she whispered raspingly. "Just wait until you drag me to that precious ranch of yours—the heat and exhaustion might just do the job for you." He released her immediately and stepped back, raking his fingers through his hair, and she pressed trembling hands against her throat. They simply stared at each other until with a muffled exclamation Ryan turned away.

They said nothing more to each other until Jonathan had been fed and Devon had tucked him into the crib in her bedroom. After switching off the light, she tiptoed back into the sitting room only to find Ryan poised by the suite's double doors, his jacket flung over one shoulder.

"I've ordered dinner," he muttered, his expression dark and unreadable as his eyes swept over her. "They said it would be sent up about six fifteen. I should be back by then. I'm just going out to make a call."

Before Devon had any chance to respond, he was out the door and gone. A sudden chill of loneliness moved down her spine, and she wrapped her arms tightly around her chest as she walked to the sofa to sink wearily down on a brocade cushion. There was a perfectly good phone in the suite that he could have used to make his call. Unless he planned to have a very private conversation that he didn't want her to overhear. It was Iris he was calling; suddenly Devon was as certain of that as she had ever been certain of anything in her life. And there was nothing at all she could do about it.

Dinner did indeed arrive around six fifteen. Unfortunately, Ryan had not yet returned, and Devon refused to begin eating without him. Both of them had acted like barbarians today. She would at least be civilized and wait for him to join her for dinner.

The minutes ticked by with excruciating slowness. Finally, at seven o'clock, she decided he was not coming back for dinner at all. She pulled herself up from the sofa and went to lift the silver cover off one of the dishes that had been arranged on a small round table, grimacing at the sight of the cold braised steak and steamed vegetables. Ah, well, she hadn't been very hungry anyway, she thought with a rueful little smile as she went back to fling herself face down on the sofa. All she wanted was to go to sleep if only for a few minutes to escape the suspicion that Ryan had not gone to call Iris at all but instead had gone to meet her somewhere. Perhaps she had come to town for just such a secret rendezvous. Tortured by the probability that the two of them were together right at that very moment, Devon impatiently brushed a tear from her cheek and buried her face in the pillow of her folded arms.

She was half awakened by the strange sensation of floating up in the air; oddly enough, it was not a sensation that frightened her. Her eyelids partially opened then flickered shut again as she realized Ryan was carrying her somewhere. Too drowsy to think, she slipped her arm around his neck, snuggling closer to the hard warmth of his chest.

"What time is it?" she murmured sleepily.

"Seven thirty," he whispered, his breath hot against her forehead. "Time for all tired little girls to be in bed."

Devon yawned and pushing halfheartedly at his chest with her free hand, she shook her head.

"Can't go to bed yet. Jonathan will wake up in a minute, then I have to give him his ten o'clock feeding."

"You let me worry about Jonathan tonight," Ryan commanded, carrying her into the bedroom. "I'll entertain him until ten o'clock, then I'll feed him. All you need do is stay in this bed and get some extra sleep."

Though Devon murmured a soft protest as she was put down on the cool satin sheet of her bed, she could not prevent her blinking eyelids from closing completely against the glare of the overhead light. Even when Ryan eased off her blouse and skirt, she could not rouse herself from her sleepiness enough to insist he stop.

"You didn't have any of your dinner," Ryan chided gently a moment later as he pulled the bedclothes up around her shoulders. "You should've eaten something, Devon."

"I was waiting for you," she mumbled, nuzzling her cheek against the pillow. "You didn't come. But I wasn't hungry, anyway."

"Devon, Devon," he whispered. "What am I going to do with you?"

"What would you like to do?" she whispered back, but before he could even begin to answer, she had drifted into a deep, dreamless sleep.

At seven o'clock the next morning, Devon was awakened by Jonathan, who was howling loudly for his breakfast. Before she could get out of bed to go to him, however,

Ryan opened the bedroom door and started into the room, only stopping when he saw her sitting up in the center of the bed, clutching the blue satin sheet around her.

"I was hoping you could sleep a little longer," he explained, cutting his eyes toward their son. "But I see little loudmouth couldn't keep quiet until I could come in here and get him."

"Babies aren't generally known for their patience," Devon said wryly, pushing her tousled hair back from her face. "Besides, he slept later today than he usually does, so I can't complain. He must have been very tired too."

"Well, actually, I kept him up awhile after his ten o'clock feeding last night," Ryan admitted sheepishly. "I was watching him play in front of that mirror and just lost track of the time."

A slight answering smile tugged at the corners of Devon's mouth, but as something barely discernible and totally indefinable suddenly darkened his eyes she instinctively drew the sheet up under her chin.

"Why don't you take Jonathan into the sitting room while I shower and get dressed," she suggested hastily, her cheeks warming as a swift knowing smile flashed on his tan face. As he gathered up their son and left the room without another word, she watched him go, conflicting emotions etching a tiny frown on her brow. How could he be so nice sometimes, so irresistibly tender, then change without warning to a ruthless, vindictive stranger who apparently found a perverse delight in making her feel as miserable as he possibly could? To her he seemed completely unpredictable and therefore infinitely dangerous.

Maybe he was being torn by conflicting emotions too, Devon considered as she went into the adjoining bathroom for a quick, coolly refreshing shower. Though he obviously felt a responsibility for his son and maybe even for her, perhaps he also resented the disruption they had caused in his life. The entire situation had to be difficult for him, she told herself as she slipped into a white cotton blouse and a faded blue corded skirt. She stepped into her navy espadrilles, then walked over to stand before the mirror, grimacing at her reflection as she rubbed a tiny amount of blusher onto her pale cheeks. As she brushed her hair with firm even strokes she tried to bring herself to the point of understanding how he must feel, but she could not quite accomplish such a magnanimous feat. After all, she had no desire to be in Texas, even for Jonathan's sake. If Ryan was disappointed now because his future with Iris had been postponed, he should not take his resentment out on her. Though she would never admit to him how much he had hurt her, he should be sensitive enough to realize to some extent how devastating his desertion had been. Now, at the very least, he should force himself to treat her decently despite his resentment.

He *should* treat her decently, but would he? Probably not, Devon decided as she walked to the door and hovered there uncertainly for a few moments. The never-ceasing empty ache in her chest sharpened abruptly. Sighing heavily, she allowed her shoulders to sag for a fraction of a second, then straightened them determinedly. No matter how often Ryan took his frustrations out on her, she had to survive this ordeal with some of her self-esteem intact, if only for Jonathan's sake. Ryan had accused her of trying to act tough, but she really had no other choice. Whenever he chose to taunt and to torment her, she had to try to remain aloof, and whenever he chose to treat her with tenderness, she could not allow herself to be overwhelmed with thoughts of what might have been. Better yet, she could try to spend as little time as possible with him, thus avoiding being subjected to both his mockery and his tenderness. That meant she must resist the temptation to stay near him simply because he was the only person she knew in this entire state. No matter how lonely she felt, no matter how his nearness affected her, she had to convince him she did not need to be with him. Taking a deep

breath, she opened her bedroom door. Today was as good a day as any to begin convincing him.

Ryan had altogether different plans for the day, however. The moment Devon entered the sitting room, he escorted her to the small round table, where their breakfast had been set out.

"But I have to feed Jonathan first," she protested, easing her elbow from his firm grip. "I'm surprised he's not squalling now, after waiting this long to eat."

"I'll have you know I'm not quite the incompetent father you think I am," Ryan said, shaking his head in mock admonition. "Your son has already downed his breakfast with his usual greed and is now lying contentedly on the floor, admiring himself in the mirror."

Sitting down automatically in the chair Ryan pulled out for her, Devon gazed up at him with some amazement.

"You fed him yourself without any trouble?" she asked, her tone frankly doubtful. "You mean, he didn't let cereal roll out of his mouth onto your shirt or anything?"

Ryan chuckled softly as he sat down at the table across from her. "We both actually managed to stay pretty clean this morning. Of course, we'd practiced last night and that was a different story. Do you happen to know if strained plums leave a stain? If so, my white shirt is now polka dot."

"Oh, I'm sorry," she murmured. "I should have gotten up and fed him myself last night."

"Don't be silly," Ryan said matter-of-factly, reaching over to lift the silver cover off her plate. "You obviously needed the extra sleep. You don't get enough rest, Devon, just as you don't make yourself eat enough. You're very thin."

Devon looked down in dismay at the rashers of bacon and the eggs and hot buttered toast on her plate.

"I won't be very thin long if I eat all that. There's much too much of everything. I'll never be able to eat it all."

"Try," was Ryan's terse command.

Feeling as if he were watching every forkful that she put in her mouth, she did eat as much as she possibly could but balked at the last two strips of bacon and squares of toast. Perhaps it was nerves, but she simply could not swallow another bite. Finally, she folded her napkin and tucked it beneath the edge of the plate.

"Can't you finish it all, Devon?" Ryan asked gently. "It really wasn't all that much to eat."

Recognizing that dangerously tender tone, she fought the desire to succumb to his coaxing. With a nonchalant shrug, she forced what she hoped seemed a bright smile. "I don't want to get fat, Ryan. I ate enough."

Without smiling in return, he shook his head. "No, you didn't, and since you obviously haven't been eating enough for quite some time, it's a good thing I got you a doctor's appointment for this morning."

"You didn't!" Devon's hands clenched into fists on the tabletop. "Now why did you do that, Ryan? I'm not sick. I certainly don't need to see a doctor!"

"You just don't realize how pale and thin you are, do you?" he responded calmly but with a no-nonsense glint in his eyes. "I think you should have a doctor look you over."

"But I saw my obstetrician about two months ago, and he said I'd be fine as long as I took care of myself."

"Which you haven't been doing, have you?"

"For goodness' sake, do I look that awful?" she countered defensively. "Personally, I don't think I'm all that thin, and I'd appreciate if you'd stop telling me I am. I'm not sick and I'm not going to see a doctor."

"Oh, yes, you are, Devon," Ryan muttered, pinning her wrist to the table with strong, hard fingers when she started to stand. "I've made the appointment and intend to see that you keep it."

Devon sniffed. "Didn't the receptionist think it was rather odd that a man was making the appointment for me?"

"Not really." Ryan grinned. "I just told her I was your husband. That simplified everything. Just remember they'll be calling you Mrs. Wilder."

Devon bristled visibly. "Really, Ryan, you had no right to. . . ."

"But I did it. And that's that."

As she tried to twist free of his viselike grip without success, she glared at him. "You can't make me go," she muttered defiantly. "You just can't make me."

Something suspiciously like amusement danced in his blue eyes. "I never knew what a little hellcat you could be," he commented, unsuccessfully fighting a grin. "But I think you better remember that I'm much bigger than you and stronger, and if need be I'll carry you to the doctor over my shoulder."

"With me screaming and kicking and causing quite a scene?" she countered skeptically. "I don't think you would."

Ryan shrugged. "Try me."

Flopping back in her chair, Devon stared at him, wondering if she would be wise to take his threat seriously. He *was* unpredictable. Perhaps, instead of issuing challenges, she should try reasoning with him.

"What would I do with Jonathan?" she asked, examining her fingernails. "He can get very cranky in the waiting room of a doctor's office."

"Then we won't take him with us. There's no need to, anyway. This hotel provides a very reliable baby-sitting service."

Damn him! He had an answer for everything, Devon thought crossly, slinging her legs around to the side of the chair and jerking herself up to stand over him. He also stood up, towering over her and effectively reclaiming the advantage of height. She drew a long, shuddering breath of pure frustration, touching light fingertips to her temples.

"I don't want to go to a doctor and I don't see why I

69

should have to," she murmured almost petulantly, shaking her head. "No, I refuse to go and you can't make me." And when Ryan only laughed softly, she lifted her chin without a word, then flounced away from him into her bedroom.

An hour and a half later, Devon left the doctor's examining room, her face tight with disgust. The visit had been as worthless as she had expected it to be. Dr. Turner had told her nothing her own obstetrician in Boston hadn't told her two months ago, get more rest, try to eat more, take vitamins—the same old monotonous story. Of course, Dr. Turner *had* warned her not to have another child for at least another year because of her weakened emotional and physical states. But he'd stressed that if her emotional health improved, she could have another baby in the next year with no complications. Then he instructed her in the various methods of birth control. Startled by the absurdity of the entire situation, Devon hadn't been able to speak for several seconds. Then she found her tongue again and managed to pretend that her contraceptive needs had already been provided for and assured the doctor that she planned to postpone another pregnancy a few years.

As she reached the door that opened to the waiting room, she stopped a moment, straightening her skirt, and a sudden bitter smile twisted her lips. Birth control, hah! That was a laugh. The last thing in the world she needed was a quickie course in contraception. Smoothing her hair, she pushed open the door. At her entrance into the waiting room, Ryan got up from his chair in the far corner, an incongruous, overwhelmingly masculine figure in the crowd of pregnant women who sat bunched up on the couches on each side of him.

Devon hurried across the room to him, eager to escape the doctor's office and get back to Jonathan. Instead of starting for the outer door, Ryan motioned her to the chair he had just vacated.

70

"I want to speak to Dr. Turner myself," he announced quietly as she hesitated. And ignoring the flashing of resentment in her green eyes, he strode back into the doctor's domain.

Twenty minutes later, as Devon and Ryan walked out of the tall office building into the bright sunshine, she still had not spoken one word to him. Frustration and resentment were mounting rapidly in her, and she did not dare say anything at all for fear she would lose control of her temper and lash out at him on the street. But when they returned to the privacy of their hotel suite, she certainly planned to tell him a thing or two! He was trying to take over her life and she wouldn't stand for it! He didn't even love her, so what right did he have to tell her what to do? None! Oh, she planned to tell him that in no uncertain terms!

Once again, however, Ryan had different plans. As they got into the taxi he had hailed, he gave the driver the name of a restaurant as their destination. Settling herself in the far corner of the backseat, Devon heaved an irritated sigh. "Would you have the driver drop me off at the hotel before you go on?" she requested stiffly. "I'd like to get back to Jonathan now, if you don't mind."

Turning his head, he allowed his curiously solemn gaze to wander over her, then looked away again. "I'm afraid I do mind. We're having lunch before we do anything else."

"But I'm not hungry at all!"

"Then you better start getting hungry, because you are going to eat even if I have to hold you on my lap and force every single bite into your mouth."

Recognizing the grim determination in his voice, Devon subsided into her corner in a silent rage that became panicky despair. Why couldn't he just leave her alone? It wasn't fair that he was turning her life upside down again. She had only wanted to put him far back in her memory where he could no longer cause her such excruciating pain.

The restaurant overlooked one of Texas's prettiest public beaches. Devon sat across from Ryan at a table by a plate-glass window and gazed wistfully at a group of young people playing with a beach ball on the sparkling sand. Beyond them sunbathers lay scattered on blankets. A few hardy souls were swimming in the blue waters of the Gulf, which surprised Devon. After all, it was still only May.

"Isn't the water too cool this time of year for swimming?" she asked curiously. "Or isn't it ever too cool?"

"Not until mid-winter usually," Ryan answered, smiling slightly at the wistful expression in her eyes. "You like to swim, don't you, Devon?" When she nodded, he smiled encouragingly. "Good. We have a pool at the ranch, so anytime you want to you'll be able to take a swim."

Devon only sighed.

"You don't want to go, do you?" he prompted softly. "You think the ranch is going to be a terrible place?"

"I like places with water somewhere close by. Heat . . . heat can be so oppressive."

"Yes, but the ranch will grow on you in time, if you'll let it. It can be very beautiful there, especially at night. The land stretches out silent and shadowed under the stars, and far off in the distance you can see the mountains' purple silhouette against the dark-blue sky."

"I like places with water," Devon repeated softly, bending her head, unwilling to look at him. "Water is so soothing and cool."

"Yes, well, I'd take you swimming today, but it's really not all that warm, and you look so damned frail sometimes I'd be afraid you'd catch . . ." His words trailed off, then suddenly his hand reached out to cover the much smaller one that rested on the table. "My God, Devon, why didn't you tell me what a bad time you had when Jonathan was born? All those hours in labor . . . God, you should have told me!"

"It's over now, so why talk about it? I try not to think about it at all."

"Was . . . was Andrews with you? Did he stay with you during . . ."

"Ben died over two months before Jonathan was born, Ryan. I thought you knew that."

"Then you mean no one was with you? You went through it all alone?"

"It wasn't so bad, really," she murmured. "The doctors and nurses were all very nice to me." When Ryan groaned, her eyes darted up just in time to see a fleeting expression of anguish cross his face.

"It shouldn't have been that way," he rasped. "You must have been so scared, going through that alone."

"I survived," she said, attempting flippancy to negate her disturbing response to his tenderness. She eased her hand out from beneath his. "Could we talk about something else, please? Anything else."

They talked very little at all, however, during the next thirty minutes, and by the time lunch ended Devon was more eager than ever to return to the hotel.

"I bet Jonathan has missed me . . . us," she said as Ryan escorted her from the restaurant. "I just hope he wasn't upset at having a strange baby-sitter."

"I'm sure he's just fine," Ryan reassured her as they got into a taxi. "And he'll be just fine for a few more hours while we go shopping for some new clothes for you."

"Clothes! But I don't want any new clothes. I have all I need."

"And all of them are old and too big for you now. You're getting a whole new wardrobe."

Oh, no, I'm not, she thought bitterly. Maybe he did feel guilty because she had been all alone when Jonathan was born but he was not going to assuage that guilt by making

73

her his favorite charity. She would walk around in rags before she would let him buy her off with clothes.

"I'm really too tired to go shopping," she finally told him. "Maybe some other time."

"You're not tired, Devon; you're just incredibly stubborn," he responded calmly. "And we are going shopping today."

"I won't look at the clothes," she argued tersely. "I won't even go with you into the stores."

"Like you didn't go with me to the doctor?" he asked mockingly.

And with that pithy reminder, she knew he had defeated her once again.

At ten thirty that evening, as Devon secured the tie belt of her faded and frayed green robe, she stared at all the new clothes hanging in her closet and shook her head. Ryan certainly had been extravagant despite her continued protests. Besides jeans, skirts, and blouses, he had insisted she buy two long dresses for evening, one a forest-green jersey blend and the other a ridiculously expensive white crochet that looked as if it had come from some more romantic era. It was lovely, she had to admit, and delightfully feminine. Where would she wear something so fancy, she had asked him. Out to round up the cattle? But he had only smiled secretively and told the salesclerk they would take the dress.

Still shaking her head, Devon wandered into the bathroom to brush her teeth, then realized with a grimace that there was no toothpaste. The new tube she had bought today was still in her purse, which she had left in the sitting room. Tightening her belt, she walked back through her bedroom, stopping by Jonathan's crib to pull his blanket up over him again. Ryan had been right, she thought rather sheepishly as she went on into the sitting room. The baby had survived his hours with a strange sitter without any sign of trauma.

74

She found her purse on the sofa where she had left it, but as she slung it over her shoulder and started back for her room, Ryan's bedroom door opened and he stepped out. His unbuttoned shirt revealed the tan expanse of his muscular chest. Devon had to drag her gaze away from the flat tenseness of his stomach.

"I thought I'd have a drink," he explained, coming closer. "Would you like one, too?"

"N . . . no, thank you," she murmured, trying to ignore the sudden thudding of her heart. Why did he have to appear so overwhelmingly attractive now, at this time of night? Jonathan was sound asleep. It suddenly seemed to Devon that they were isolated from the rest of the world in this little room, just the two of them. If only he loved her and this were a real marriage, she thought fleetingly, then pushed such hopeless longings from her mind. Half-turning away, she sighed. "I'm going to bed. Good night, Ryan."

With two long strides he was beside her, catching her shoulder to turn her back around.

"Wait just a minute," he commanded, his eyes dark. "Why are you still wearing this tattered old robe? Don't you like the new one we bought you today?"

Riveting her eyes on his chiseled chin, she shook her head. "I couldn't throw this one away. I mean, I like the new one—it's very pretty—but this one is . . . is so comfortable, like an old friend."

"You have to be the most stubborn human being I've ever met in my entire life," he chided softly. "Now, I'm going to take this robe and throw it away, and you're going to go put on the new one and show me how it looks."

Before Devon could react, he reached out and with a quick jerk on one end of the robe's tie belt undid it completely. His strong hands crushed the soft fabric of her lapels.

"No!" she gasped, frantically trying to pry his fingers loose. "Don't, Ryan! I . . . I don't have anything on underneath!" He stood perfectly still for a moment and she gazed up into his narrowing eyes, feeling suddenly lost in their dark depths. Though her breath caught, she could make no move to stop him as he slowly, very slowly, pulled open the robe. She heard his sharp intake of breath, and as his gaze wandered over her, her legs went weak beneath her and she tightened her grip on his strong wrists just to keep her balance.

"Oh, God, Devon!" he whispered hoarsely. "You're so beautiful. And I want you! God, how I *want* you!" Dragging her to him, pulling her arms up around his neck, he encircled her waist with strong, squeezing hands. His mouth sought and found hers, parting the soft fullness of her lips with the fierce demand of his.

It seemed as if it had been forever since he had kissed her this way. Devon was unable to control her body's traitorous response. Stretching up on tiptoe, she strained against him, the soft curves of her body yielding to the hard, muscular line of his. Her arms around his neck tightened as she gave him back kiss for kiss, her mouth opening to the irresistibly tender demand of his. As Ryan's hands slid down to cover her bare hips and press her hard against the hardening strength of his thighs, she moaned softly, remembering. Then his lips were down her neck, down to the full, firm curve of her breast, to the taut, straining peak. As he teased the sensitive skin with the tip of his tongue, she twined her fingers in his hair, her breath coming in quick gasps.

"Delicious!" he whispered. "You smell and taste delicious. You always did."

A quickening need flared to life within Devon. His touch and the endearments he whispered kindled wildfires that danced over every inch of her skin. The searching kisses Ryan trailed upward over her collarbone, then the creamy curve of her neck created both torture and ecstasy. As her lips parted eagerly in surrender, his hands slid down her back, molding her gently rounded hips, drawing her to him. Feminine instinct older than the ages compelled her to move against him, and as she did, he swept her up into his arms and strode toward the doorway to his bedroom.

Beyond resistance in the seclusion of the lamplit room, Devon clung weakly to his shoulders, her eyes closed as he lowered her to her feet. Feeling the edge of the bed behind her knees, she trembled as he removed her robe and it drifted with a whisper to the floor around her bare feet. Yet she became all warm, feminine acquiescence when Ryan picked her up again, this time to put her gently on his bed.

The sheets cooled her burning naked skin, but couldn't diminish the fire of desire that flared within. Her eyes flickered open, dark emerald and drowsy with passion, as Ryan swiftly stripped his own clothes off, then lay down beside her. When she involuntarily tensed, he turned her toward him.

"Devon, relax," he coaxed softly. "This time I won't hurt you." When she reached out to him, inviting his lovemaking, he murmured her name again and again and drew her closer, plundering her mouth with ever-deepening kisses.

Devon's feverish response heightened his need of her. Breathing swiftly and unsteadily, he at last released her mouth only to lower his head. Firm, gently pulling lips closed around first one, then the other of the pulsating peaks of her breasts. His tongue tasted the tightening, hardening nubs, and when he tenderly nibbled at them and she shivered ecstatically, his fingers traced around the nipples and massaged downward along the slopes of firm yet femininely pliant flesh. When every silken inch of her breasts had been touched and tasted, his caresses became more intimate, demanding everything of her. Now she was willing to give anything he demanded. Lost in the spellbinding sensations his touch evoked, she sighed with satisfaction as his firm lips grazed across her abdomen. Her spiraling senses were caught up in the exquisite tide of his passion and her own, until she was swept irrevocably into a world of sensual pleasures.

Devon's only coherent thought was that she loved Ryan still. She had never stopped loving him, and knowing that now she longed to belong completely to him again.

Her lips clung to his when he kissed her again, opening to the tongue that sought the sweetness within her mouth. Tracing the taut, muscular contours of his back, she inhaled his fresh, masculine scent. And when his gentle hand stroked the sensitized inner flesh of her thighs, she arched upward. With a triumphant murmur, Ryan covered her body with his, easing down to her compelling warmth, his lips capturing her soft moan of passion as he began to move slowly against her until nothing in the world existed except themselves and the wonder their bodies could create together.

Hours later, after they had made love a second time, Devon lay close to Ryan, her head nestled in the warm hollow of his shoulder. The feel of his skin brushing hers was heavenly, and for the first time in a year she felt totally relaxed and happy. After the hours she and Ryan had just shared, she dared to hope everything actually could work out happily for them. She loved him so completely. Knowing that at least she could fully satisfy his physical desires, she thought perhaps he might begin to love her in return someday. She had to hope for that, even believe it, considering how fervently she had just given herself to him again.

Warm and content, Devon lay quietly, feeling Ryan's heartbeat slow beneath her hand. After a few minutes, she breathed a tremulous sigh. Ryan was very still beside her, so still that she thought he must have fallen asleep. She smiled. Very gently, she kissed his bronze skin where it hardened over his collarbone. "Oh, Ryan," she whispered.

"God, Devon, I'm sorry," he suddenly groaned, unaware he had startled her by speaking. "I'm so sorry. I never meant for this to happen."

Devon stiffened. Pain exploded like raw fire in her chest. He sounded so contrite, so *ashamed!* She shrank away from him, humiliation washing over her. He was sorry tonight had happened! She hadn't been sorry at all, but he was. She could hardly bear knowing that.

Excruciating pain seemed to knot her muscles, but she forced herself to respond. "No need to apologize," she muttered, miraculously steadying the tremor in her voice. "These things . . . just happen sometimes, I guess."

"But, Devon," he began raggedly, "if I've made you pregnant again . . ."

"Oh, surely you won't be so unlucky a second time," she retorted with vehement sarcasm, slipping quickly from his bed and grabbing her robe off the floor. Rushing to the door, she flung back at him, "And even if I am pregnant again, you won't have to feel any responsibility. I can take care of myself."

Scarcely aware he was calling after her, Devon walked unsteadily across the sitting room to her bedroom. Stifling a sob, she swiftly locked the door behind her, then ran to fling herself across her own bed. Tears filled her eyes and spilled onto her cheeks. She muffled the soft sound of her crying in her pillow. What a fool she was! What a stupid, stupid fool! Even the past year hadn't taught her a lesson. She had let Ryan use her then, and tonight she had let him use her again. She simply had no common sense. She couldn't have any if she had believed she could control her emotions where Ryan was concerned. She had actually thought she could be indifferent!

CHAPTER FIVE

The flight to Wilder Ranch was not particularly pleasant. The gleaming, white six-seater Cessna ran into turbulence, and with every shudder and sudden drop in altitude, Devon cringed and tightened her arms around her sleeping son. Compared to the mammoth jetliner that had delivered them safely to Corpus Christi two days ago, this tiny aircraft seemed eggshell fragile. Even with Ryan's steady hands on the controls, Devon felt much less than secure. He and Luke Bishop, the foreman from the ranch, however, did not seem at all disturbed by the turbulence.

Of course, Luke Bishop had impressed Devon from the beginning as a man who let little disturb him. Every movement he made was unhurried and deliberate, and very little emotion played on his lined brown face. On meeting him, though, Devon had caught what seemed a tiny glimmer of disapproval as his squinting gray eyes flicked over her. Luke didn't talk much, at least not to her, and she had the feeling he saw her as an interloper, a girl who had crashed into Ryan's life and caused him considerable inconvenience.

Propping her elbow on the seat's armrest, Devon rested her chin in her cupped hand, staring bleakly out the window at the azure sky. During the past two days, she had spent all her waking moments trying to cope with Ryan's resentment toward her. There had been no time to consider the possibility that almost everyone at the ranch might resent her as he did. Now, with the moment of truth rapidly approaching, she wished she had considered that possibility. Then she might have been able to steel herself against all the mocking glances and perhaps even downright unfriendliness that could be awaiting her arrival.

Without thinking, she released her breath in a long, tremulous sigh, then blushed hotly as both pilot and co-pilot glanced back at her. Flustered, she pretended to be quite involved with straightening the thin cotton blanket that covered Jonathan's legs, but her eyes darted up again as Luke coughed politely to gain her attention.

"Cup of coffee, miss?" he offered solemnly, holding up a steaming cup. "From a thermos, but it's better than nothing."

Tightened into a knot by nerves and jostled by the bumpy flight, her stomach rebelled at the very idea of coffee. A slight nausea rose in her, but she managed to muster a wan smile.

"I . . . No. No, thank you, Luke."

"Suit yourself," he said with a shrug, turning to offer the cup to the younger man. "Ryan?"

As the men talked quietly for a few minutes, Devon closed her eyes and rested her head back against the seat, comparing the distinct drawl in Luke's voice to the less jarring one in Ryan's. It had been that deep, resonant, melodious voice that had first drawn her to Ryan, and as she recalled the evening she had attended his lecture and their eyes had met so frequently, a rueful smile curved her lips. She could never have imagined then that such an inauspicious beginning would lead her into her present situation. Perhaps if she had been more experienced, it never would have. She hadn't exactly been a woman of the world. Caught up in her desire to become a writer, she'd allotted very little time for a social life. Now as she looked back on it all, she had to wonder what Ryan had ever seen in her. Her bitterness wanted to conclude that he had simply realized how easy it would be to seduce her, but despite all the pain she had felt in the past year, she could not quite accept that conclusion. He had felt something for her in the beginning, at least, even if it had been no more than a fascination for her naiveté. Unfortunately, that fascination hadn't lasted, though she had remained painfully naive. Obviously she had, or Ryan's threat to sue for custody would never have astounded her the way it had. Ah, but she was getting wiser, she told herself, as she brushed a lock of Jonathan's dark hair back from his smooth forehead.

"You're very quiet back here," Ryan suddenly said, interrupting her thoughts as he eased his way between the forward seats and sat down in the one next to her. As he reached out to touch a gentle fingertip to the tiny toe that was peeking out from beneath the blanket, he smiled and transferred some of the warmth of that gaze to her when his eyes drifted from the baby to her face. "You seem to have a lot on your mind. Care to share your thoughts?"

"Not really," she replied tightly, unable to look directly at him. "I was just sort of daydreaming."

Ryan's expression became at once disturbed and disturbing. "Devon, if you're upset about last night, I . . ."

"Forget last night." Swallowing with difficulty, she attempted a careless toss of one hand. "Just forget what happened. I intend to."

After a long, tense silence, he shrugged. "Whatever you say. So if that's not what's bothering you, what is? Surely you're not dreading your stay at the ranch all this much? You shouldn't, you know. You haven't exactly been sent into exile in Siberia."

The next thing to it, she wanted to retort, but didn't. Part of wisdom was knowing it was a mistake to make disparaging remarks about the land a man loved. And Ryan obviously loved this land, though from what Devon had been able to see from the plane, she wasn't at all sure why.

"Better give yourself a chance, Devon," he continued

rather harshly. With one lean finger, he tilted her chin up, turning her face toward him. "And give this place a chance. As I told you yesterday, West Texas can be very beautiful, and since you're going to be here for a while . . ."

"How is all this going to end, Ryan?" she exclaimed abruptly in a whisper, dark uncertainty filling her eyes. "How long are you going to want Jonathan with you? How long will you want us to stay?"

Some strange emotion played across his face, then was gone. "I really don't know how long. Why? Are you *that* eager to end it?"

"Aren't you?" she snapped back defensively. "After all, you're the one who has a fiancée to come along behind and pick up the pieces."

His hard fingers clamped her chin. "But *you're* my fiancée, darling," he calmly informed her. "Since I still think it would be wise for us to get married, I'm considering us engaged. After all, you've had my baby and I am bringing you both home with me. People will expect us to have made some kind of commitment."

"Well, I didn't ask you to stage this charade, just you remember that," she retorted, jerking her head back to free herself of his hold. "So if you're having second thoughts now, don't blame me. It was all your idea. Be sure to tell your precious Iris that. Then maybe she won't try to sneak up on me some night while I'm here and murder me in my sleep for ruining all her plans with you."

"Don't be ridiculous, Devon," he muttered disgustedly. "Iris isn't—"

"I think we should set a time," Devon interrupted, not wanting to hear what Iris was or wasn't. "Actually, it shouldn't take long, do you think? How about three months?"

For a moment he simply stared at her, the pulse in his right temple beating with fascinatingly rapid regularity. Then a mocking smile twisted his lips as he shook his head. "No way, Devon. I plan to share more of Jonathan's infancy than that. You'll have to stay a year at least, preferably as my wife."

"A year!" she gasped, her face paling. "But I'd never be able to stand it here that long!" She *wouldn't* be able to, especially not as his wife. He couldn't force her to marry him; she wouldn't let him. It was difficult enough to contemplate simply living on the ranch for a whole year, loving Ryan, yet not being loved in return. . . . She could hardly bear to think about it. Hoping for a compromise, she offered, "Six months."

"Nine."

"Seven."

"Nine, Devon, and that's final," he whispered roughly. "Now, take it without another word or I swear to God I'll insist on a year."

How ironic, she thought, suspended halfway between tears and bitter laughter, unable to seek release from her unhappiness in either. Nine months again. After a pregnancy, nine months took on a connotation for a woman that a man couldn't possibly understand, especially after a pregnancy like hers had been—long days and nights of loneliness and fears of what the future would be for her child and for herself. Now to even think of having to endure nine more months of such tortuous uncertainty was almost more than she could stand. Her hand fluttered out to hover above Ryan's khaki-clad arm, but she didn't touch him.

"But . . . but that's so long," she began haltingly. "Iris won't want to wait all those months. And I . . . I have to start a life for Jonathan and me, the sooner the better. Let me go home."

"Home?" His dark brows lifted. "I hope you don't mean Boston, Devon, because that's out of the question. If you choose to leave the ranch, the farthest you'll be able to go is Corpus Christi, surely you realize that. I couldn't be much of a father to my son if you took him a thousand miles away."

"But you can't keep me here against my will," she whispered incredulously. "If I decide to go back to Boston, you can't do a thing to stop me."

Heaving an impatient sigh, Ryan massaged the back of his neck. "You're right. I can't stop *you* from leaving me or from leaving Texas, but I can stop you from taking my son with you. If I petition the court—"

"Oh, just shut up!" she exclaimed plaintively, not caring whether Luke heard as her voice broke on a soft sob of defeat. Turning from Ryan, she pressed her hand against her abdomen, feeling more than a little nauseated. When his fingers suddenly brushed her bare forearm, she pulled away, uttering a little cry. "You and your damn courts . . . you . . . you and . . ."

"For God's sake, Devon, why do you keep pushing me into these corners?" he muttered angrily. "Do you think I enjoy threatening you this way? I don't, but you give me no choice. Can't you just try a little harder to give this arrangement a chance? If you try, maybe . . ."

"Oh, leave me alone," she murmured, pressing the heel of her hand against her forehead, unable to respond to the hint of appeal she thought she detected in his voice. All she could feel at that moment was a barely controllable panic at the thought of living nine months in the same house with him, loving him more every day and having to watch him dally about with his Iris, who from what he had said lived practically within touching distance. Taking a deep, shuddering breath, she fought to overcome that panic. She could get through the next nine months; she had to. She could do it if she remembered to take one long day at a time, just as she had done during her pregnancy. Having resigned herself to the situation to some extent, she was able to meet Ryan's watchful gaze.

"All right, you've won again," she said dully. "But if we

stay at the ranch the nine months, you will l . . . let me take Jonathan home then, won't you?"

His eyes darkened to blue again as they searched her face, then his breath whistled through clenched teeth.

"He is my son, too, Devon. And you're sadly mistaken if you think I can ever forget that."

That meant no; he wouldn't let them go back to Boston in nine months. It was totally beyond Devon's capabilities to face that realization now. Her mind felt numb, incapable of forming coherent thoughts. She simply stared blankly at Ryan, unaware of the lost, bewildered look in her eyes.

"Don't waste that wounded look on me," he commanded furiously, raising his hand almost as if he longed to hit her, then letting it drop again. "I won't let you make me feel like the world's biggest son of a . . ." Shaking his head, he began again: "Look, can't we try to make something decent out of this situation? I know you enjoy hating me, but . . ."

"Hating you?" she muttered tearfully, twisting a corner of Jonathan's blanket around her forefinger as conflicting emotions tugged at her. Hate wasn't one of them. If only she could hate him, life would be so much simpler. But she knew she couldn't even pretend that what she felt for him was anything akin to hatred. Last night had proved that love didn't die so easily, though she wished desperately that it did.

Too overwrought to say another word, she turned to stare blindly out the window, then felt a renewed sense of loss as Ryan immediately moved up to take the controls again.

Obviously, Luke had heard most or all of the emotional discussion, because he made no effort to engage Ryan in conversation. In the long, uncomfortable silence that followed, Devon sat tensed in her seat, cradling Jonathan in her arms. Far below, the seemingly endless expanse of plain shimmered red in the bright midafternoon sunlight, ribboned by a network of small creeks and rivers, which glinted silver as their waters reflected the sun's rays. Vegetation edged the streams; tall cottonwood trees towered above an undergrowth of scrubby mesquite and provided an illusion of coolness in what otherwise seemed to Devon a vast, hot, sparsely grassy sweep of nothingness. Though she could not deny that Texas was beautiful with its rich, earthy colors and sun-withered, gently rolling hills, it seemed to her that its beauty was desolate and forbidding. She would have been quite content to admire it from a distance and to leave its mysteries to the more adventuresome types. It made her far too uneasy. Even high above it, she felt imprisoned by its vastness. What was she doing in this semi-desert over a thousand miles from everything she knew and understood? She shouldn't be here. She didn't belong, and she was scared.

Perhaps, she considered, she was scared because the terrain below reminded her of Ryan—beckoningly mysterious, yet potentially dangerous and completely unpredictable. To her, both the land and the man seemed harsh, yet both possessed that enticing promise of excitement, an excitement that involved great risks for anyone brave enough to seek it. And she wasn't that brave anymore. She had taken the risk once and lost badly. Now all she wanted was a sense of security, but since she would never find that here, she wished the plane could carry her all the way home to Boston where at the very least she knew she belonged.

Even as she wished, the small plane commenced a gentle descent. Holding her breath, Devon pressed her lips tightly together to stop their sudden trembling. She watched a dark cluster in the distance separate into what she soon saw were buildings. When a narrow sun-deflecting landing strip claimed her attention, she lifted Jonathan up onto her shoulder, holding him close against her. He slept on, perfectly secure in her arms. She pressed a light, loving kiss against a dark-fringed eyelid and whispered wryly, "I see you're as nervous as I am." Except for a bubbly sigh, the baby made no response. He didn't stir even an inch a few moments later as the wheels of the plane touched down with a shudder and skimmed across the surface of the smooth Tarmac, slowing to a gentle stop by a small hangar at the end of the strip.

Devon opened her eyes to find Ryan watching her, sardonic amusement slightly uplifting the corners of his mouth.

"Closing your eyes during landing indicates a lack of faith in the pilot," he drawled as he opened his door and swung out onto the ground. A few seconds later, he reached in to take Jonathan from her, still grinning. "What's the matter, Devon? Were you afraid I hadn't taken my landing lesson yet?"

Her cheeks burned, not so much from the teasing as from his method of helping her from the plane. With Jonathan in one arm, he clasped his other around her waist, lifting her out easily, then bringing her close against him before her feet could touch the ground. The heat of his body penetrated the thin cotton of her dress, and with their faces on a level she could detect the tiny lines at the corners of his eyes. Suddenly his lips brushed across hers, then covered them completely, firm and warm and enticing.

"Open your mouth, Devon," he whispered seductively. "Let me really kiss you."

To her everlasting shame, she obeyed him. Her lips parted slightly for a brief instant and the tip of his tongue began lazily to explore her mouth. She jerked away from him, terrified of being swept away by evocative memories of last night.

"Stop it, Ryan. Right now," she tried to command with icy disdain. Pushing violently at his chest, she looked all around, wondering if anyone had witnessed that kiss. No one was in sight. Except for Luke, who was removing the luggage on the other side of the plane, and a lanky yellow dog that was loping toward them, wagging a welcome, they were alone. All around them the land stretched out. It was perfectly quiet except for the rustling of the wind in the sparse grasses and scrubby bushes plus the whinny of one of the horses in a paddock between the landing strip and the group of buildings. Despite the lack of witnesses to the kiss, she struggled to free herself of Ryan's arms. "Will you put me down please before you drop Jonathan?"

"I think I can handle both of you at the same time. Neither of you weigh anything," he commented dryly as he lowered her feet to the ground. When she hastily smoothed her skirt, he shook his head. "You shouldn't be so inhibited, Devon. Why don't you try to relax?"

"Relax?" she exclaimed softly, suddenly-confused green eyes searching his face. "How can I relax? One minute you're threatening me and the next you're . . . you're . . ."

"Making love to you?" he prompted, an inexplicable gleam in his eyes. "Is that what you're trying to say?"

"Kissing me," she amended hastily, averting her gaze. "I . . . I just wish you'd be consistent. The way you keep changing moods, I never know . . . what to expect from you."

"You'll just have to learn then, won't you?" he countered confidently, taking her elbow to escort her to the cream-colored station wagon that Luke was loading luggage into.

The foreman declined to ride with Ryan and Devon, saying he wanted to walk back alongside the horse paddock to check the condition of the fencing. Devon wondered if he simply didn't want to risk becoming a reluctant listener to another argument.

"I guess I didn't make much of an impression on Luke," she said half seriously as Ryan started the station wagon, then proceeded to drive down a winding graveled drive.

"In fact, he seemed to take an instant dislike to me. Have any idea why? Did I do or say something to offend him?"

"Maybe he just disapproves of young women who marry old men for their money and influential friends," Ryan replied caustically, then lifted his broad shoulders in a careless shrug. "But why let his opinion bother you? After all, I'm sure you see him only as an ignorant Texas cowhand, right?"

"No, I most certainly do not!" Devon protested heatedly. "And if you're insinuating I'm some kind of snob—"

"If the shoe fits . . ."

"Well, it doesn't!"

"Then why are you so miserable about coming to the ranch?"

He dared ask her that! Devon suppressed the urge to smack him and instead answered honestly, though with some resentment. "I'm nervous, if you're really interested in what's wrong with me. I dread meeting your stepmother and . . ."

"Why should you dread meeting Maggie? She's a fine lady. Maybe a bit too opinionated sometimes, though she does seem somewhat subdued since Dad died. I think you should like her, even though she is a little countrified."

Devon chose to ignore his second attempt to provoke her and changed the subject instead. "Your mother— didn't you tell me last year that she remarried when you were a boy and lives in Europe now?"

"Paris."

"Do you ever see her?"

"Only if I go to Paris or meet her in New York," Ryan answered matter-of-factly. "I was a year old when she packed me up and left here. She told my father then she'd never be back, and she hasn't been. It took me from the time I was twelve until I was fourteen to persuade her to let me come visit this 'God-forsaken place,' as she always calls it."

"She hated it here that much then?"

Ryan's lean hands tightened on the steering wheel. His expression was solemn as he turned to look at Devon. "My mother was and still is a social butterfly. Of course, this place couldn't satisfy her longing for bright lights and crowds of people. She and my father should never have married; they weren't at all suited. Maybe if they'd really loved each other . . ." He shrugged. "Oh, well, just don't think you'll hate it here too because my mother did. You're not a social butterfly anyway, are you?"

"No," she answered honestly, thinking her problem might be just the opposite of what his mother's had been. As far as she was concerned, there would be one person too many close to the ranch and that person, of course, was Iris Jenkins. As Ryan stopped the car and got out to open a paddock gate, Devon nibbled her thumbnail glumly, wondering what Iris was like. The hotel clerk had said she was beautiful, but what else would she be? Sighing, Devon supposed she would soon find out. If she were in Iris's position, she would waste no time in checking out the girl Ryan had felt compelled to bring back to his home . . . to marry, even if it was only temporary.

After stopping to open two more paddock gates, Ryan drove past the first of the outlying buildings, saying it was the machine shop. As they went on, he pointed out the long structures that were the stables, a small supply store, and the bunkhouse where the cowhands stayed. There were bungalows for the cook and a mechanic and their families, then a somewhat grander one for Luke, his wife, and their four children.

It was rather like a small town, but Devon hardly noticed. Her eyes were riveted on the house that sat nestled in a grove of trees apart from the other buildings. It was nothing like she had imagined. Her mind had concocted a picture of a rather sterile-looking frame structure plopped down in the middle of nowhere with dust swirling about. But this house was lovely. Long and low, constructed of stone, it peeked out between the trunks of cottonwoods. Their pale bark and drooping heart-shaped leaves provided blessed shade. A wide screened veranda extended the entire length of the house, its stone columns festooned with moonflower vines. There was actually a garden beyond the east end, blooming with Texas bluebonnets and cultivated prairie roses.

"Disappointed?" Ryan asked as he slowed the station wagon to a stop. After switching off the engine, he half turned to her. "Well, Devon?"

"It's really beautiful, Ryan," she admitted. "I . . . I didn't expect it to look so cool. It's sort of like an oasis."

He smiled one of those slow, easy, nearly irresistible smiles and reached out to brush the back of his hand against her cheek. "An oasis, is it? Devon, you have the strangest notions. Texas isn't quite as barren as the Sahara Desert."

She had to smile, too, as he opened his door and got out, but she was nervous again by the time they walked into the house a moment later. Maggie Wilder met them in the small entrance foyer.

Ryan's stepmother was a tall woman and sturdily built, with streaks of gray in her dark-brown hair. Her clear light-hazel eyes swept over Devon without apology, then she inclined her head.

"Welcome to Wilder Ranch," she said evenly, her voice warmed by that distinctive drawl. Then she turned to Ryan, giving him a brief hug and a kiss on the cheek. "I expected you yesterday."

"The past week's been hectic," he explained easily. "All of us were tired."

"Yes, I imagine," the woman said crisply, her gaze flicking over Devon again. "Well, I'm sure you're all tired now too, so let's get your things along to your rooms. After . . ." She smiled rather sheepishly. "After I have a look at that baby." Devon pushed the edges of the cotton blanket away from Jonathan's cheek and Maggie moved closer, nodding her approval. "He's a handsome boy. Yes, very handsome."

Though the compliment was not exuberantly given, it was obviously genuine. Devon smiled her thanks, then preceded Ryan as Maggie led them down a narrow hall in the west side of the house. Jonathan's tiny room was shown first. A gleaming white crib sat against one wall; a small dresser had been painted to match. Crisp blue curtains printed with fat white teddy bears covered one wide window.

"Oh, it's lovely," Devon said enthusiastically, giving Ryan a rather relieved smile. "I . . . I didn't expect you to go to so much trouble, though."

"No trouble at all," Maggie said with a shrug. "A bit of painting and a couple of seams to run up on the sewing machine. Why don't you put the child in his bed and give your arms a rest while I show you your room."

Though Jonathan stirred slightly when he was put down in the crib, he was soon still again. Devon rubbed her cramped arms as she and Ryan followed Maggie down the hall to the next door.

"I thought Devon would like this better than your old room, Ryan," his stepmother announced, unaware of the startled glance Devon gave him. "It's so much bigger."

Devon gestured hesitantly, but as she opened her mouth to speak, Ryan caught her hand, giving it a distinct warning squeeze. "It's perfect, Maggie," he said. "Thanks."

Nodding, the older woman walked toward the door. "Devon, this end of the house will be your responsibility. When there are two women in one house, it's best to set up some kind of boundaries. That way they . . . *we* won't always be stumbling over each other's feet."

Maggie was out the door and gone before Devon could answer. A small frown knitted her brow as her eyes darted to Ryan's face, then beyond him to the huge four-poster bed that dominated the room.

"Ryan, I . . ." she began. "You . . ."

"I plan to sleep in my old room just across the hall," he cut in impatiently. "Maggie was only giving *you* this room. I doubt she was encouraging us to share a bed. So don't look as if you've been tossed into a cage with a hungry tiger." He turned away. "I'll go fetch the luggage."

"I'm sorry," she mumbled, cheeks growing hot. "But after last night . . ." Her voice trailed off as he strode from the room. Sighing, she went to peek out the door that opened onto the front veranda, then wandered across the room. To her surprise, another door opened onto a small screened porch, which extended the width of the house and overlooked a small rock garden in a clearing edged by tall trees. It was a private place, shaded and cool and fragrant, she imagined, especially when all the flowers were in bloom. But it was somewhat disconcerting to realize Ryan's room also opened onto the porch. Thoughtfully twirling a strand of hair, she wandered back into her bedroom.

Actually, the entire situation was disconcerting, though she was not really sure why it should be. Perhaps it was because this entire end of the house had been handed over to them. It was almost as if she and Ryan and Jonathan would not even be under the same roof with Maggie. The privacy seemed to make them a family. But they weren't. Yet Devon could not help wishing they could be.

To escape her disturbing thoughts, she went to check Jonathan, who was still sleeping peacefully. Then she headed down the hall toward the center of the house again, thinking she might be able to help Ryan with the luggage. She halted abruptly, however, when she heard Maggie speak her name.

"But you should know you can't expect a hothouse flower to flourish here, Ryan," Maggie Wilder was saying. "I mean, she's a pretty girl and she seems nice, but she does look so delicate. I'm not so sure she'll be able to withstand the life here."

94

"Devon's not as frail as she looks," Ryan responded patiently. "She may not be big, but she can be incredibly strong-willed."

"Hmmph, she looks plenty frail to me," his stepmother argued, though not unkindly. "I'm afraid she won't be happy here. You know your mother . . ."

"Devon won't be bored here the way Mother was, if that's what you're trying to say," Ryan interrupted rather impatiently. "You can't compare the two of them just because they're both what you might call outsiders. And besides, since the deed's done and Devon's already here, this whole discussion is pointless."

"Of course, I didn't mean . . . It's just that she doesn't look like a strong girl and . . ."

"All the more reason to take very good care of her then, don't you think? Even if I'd believed she would never adjust to life here, I could hardly leave her all alone in Boston to fend for herself, now could I?"

"Of course not; you're right, Ryan," Maggie agreed, then hastily changed the subject. "Oh, by the way, Iris has been over to visit several times since you've been away. She said to tell you . . ."

Before Maggie could finish relaying the message from Iris, Devon hurried back to her room. She did not want to hear any more, especially after what Ryan had just said. Standing before the full-length mirror attached to the closet door, she inspected her reflection carefully. She was rather thin, and the smudges of faint violet beneath her eyes did make her look somewhat fragile, she supposed. Was that the reason Ryan sometimes was nice to her? Did he simply *pity* her?

"Oh, God," she whispered bleakly at the thought. Turning from the mirror, she pressed her fingers against her lips. Suspecting he felt sorry for her was far more humiliating than believing he had only dragged her here with him because he wanted Jonathan. "I don't want your pity, Ryan," she muttered resentfully. "I don't want it and

95

I don't need it." And she didn't, she told herself, catching her lower lip between her teeth. She had been making a good life for Jonathan and herself before Ryan came along and interfered. So his pity was completely wasted on her, and she had to find some way to make him aware of that fact.

Devon hoisted one of her suitcases up onto the bed, hoping some idea might come to her while she unpacked. Before she could release the catches, Jonathan began to cry. *Poor little thing,* she thought, hurrying to the nursery. During the past few days, he had awakened in so many strange places that she feared he might be feeling very insecure by now.

"We're bouncing you from place to place like you're a ball, aren't we, sweetheart?" she said consolingly, lowering the side of his crib. As he ceased crying and began to wiggle excitedly, she smiled down at him, removing the thin sleeper he wore without much trouble despite his constant movement. After putting a dry diaper on him that she had taken from the diaper bag, she patted his chubby leg. "Well, we won't be bouncing you around any time soon, so you can think of this as home for a while. Okay?"

Blue eyes just like Ryan's gazed solemnly up at her. Then Jonathan smiled as if he had understood perfectly what she had said.

"You're such a good boy," she murmured lovingly, bending over to press a light kiss against his smooth, round abdomen. When he grasped her hair in both fists and laughed joyously, she kissed him again, delighting in the sound of his bubbly chuckle. "You have a ticklish tummy, don't you?" she said, laughing with him as she tried to ease her hair out of his strong little fingers.

"He has quite a grip, doesn't he?" Maggie said suddenly from the doorway. "Need some help getting loose?"

"I've got it now, thank you," Devon murmured as she managed to disentangle the last strand from her son's fingers. After interesting him in a small squeeze doll, she reached down to take a clean yellow terry-cloth sleeper from the bag beside her on the floor. As she dressed Jonathan in it, Maggie came and watched over the end of the crib.

"Without a doubt, he's Ryan's son," she said finally. "He looks just like him."

Though the words had been innocent enough, Devon had detected something like relief in Maggie's tone. Straightening, she looked at the older woman. "You sound as if you might have doubted he was Ryan's child before you saw him," Devon said calmly. "Did you? Have doubts, I mean?"

For a second, Maggie hesitated then nodded her head. "Yes, I had my doubts."

"Surely you knew Ryan wouldn't have gone to all the trouble of bringing Jonathan and me down here if *he'd* had any doubts. You must know he's not the kind of man who would be easily deceived in a situation like this."

"Oh, I don't know. All men can be foolish sometimes, especially when a woman is involved."

Lifting Jonathan out of his crib, Devon didn't answer. She could have easily assured Maggie she was wasting her time worrying about Ryan. He would never give any woman a chance to take advantage of him. Knowing her opinion probably wouldn't be appreciated, she simply kept it to herself as she picked up the diaper bag and started toward the door.

"Could you point me toward the kitchen, please?" she asked politely. "It's time for Jonathan to eat, and I need to warm his food."

"Oh, but why don't you let me feed him for you," Maggie offered, stepping closer as if she meant to reach for the baby. "That way you could lie down and rest while he's eating. I know you're tired. Ryan said the flight here was unusually bumpy."

Though she was exhausted and Maggie's offer was

tempting, pride made Devon shake her head. "Thank you, but I can feed him myself. I'm not all that tired."

"But you're very pale and . . ."

"Believe it or not, Mrs. Wilder, but a week ago I was working all day and taking care of Jonathan and our apartment at night all by myself," Devon declared flatly. "Actually, I was fending for myself quite well. I'm really not a fragile hothouse flower, so please don't worry about me."

"Oh, dear." Maggie sighed. "You overheard Ryan and me talking a few minutes ago, didn't you? What else did you hear?"

"Nothing much," Devon answered with a shrug. "I left when you mentioned Iris. Her message to Ryan was none of my business."

"But you obviously heard what we were saying about Ryan's mother, and I want to apologize for trying to compare you with her." Maggie grimaced. "I'm afraid I can never think about Lana with much objectivity. You see, John, Ryan's father, and I were very close when we were young. Well, to be honest, I was madly in love with him and I thought he loved me. Then he met Lana, married her, and they had Ryan. Needless to say, I was very hurt. Then it was five years after his divorce before John came back to me. All those wasted years . . . I can't help but blame Lana for them. And, well, since she was a Yankee, from up north, I mean, and you are too, I guess I unfairly compared you to her."

History was repeating itself, Devon thought, groaning inwardly. So even Maggie was going to resent her. Naturally, because of her experience with Lana years ago, she was going to sympathize with Iris Jenkins. Devon understood that, but understanding didn't make her feel any less alone.

"All I can say, Mrs. Wilder, is that I'll try not to cause anybody as many problems as Ryan's mother did," she murmured at last. "I'll really try not to."

"I was just afraid you might not be the kind of young woman who can cope with the life here. If you weren't, you'd be terribly unhappy, and that would make it difficult for everybody else. You do see what I mean, don't you?" Maggie asked hopefully. "On a ranch, a woman has to be strong."

"I can carry my own weight, I assure you," Devon said dully. "I didn't come here expecting to be pampered simply because I just had Ryan's baby. And I don't want anybody, especially Ryan, to feel I should be pampered. I'd rather stand on my own two feet."

"Then we understand each other," Maggie said, a sudden respect in her voice.

Yet Devon could gain little satisfaction from her small victory, knowing a bigger battle with Ryan was yet to come. And that was the battle she must win. If she left Texas with nothing else, she had to leave with some dignity.

CHAPTER SIX

Two days later, while Jonathan was napping, Devon went to see Ryan in the study where he attended to the business affairs of the ranch. Looking up from a hopelessly cluttered desk, he lifted questioning brows as she stood in the center of the room, her hands clasped in front of her.

"Could we talk a minute?" she asked softly. "That is, if you're not too busy."

Tossing a sheet of paper onto the disastrous desktop, he stood up, shaking his head as he answered rather sharply, "Well, I feel busy, but that doesn't seem to be getting me anywhere."

"Oh. I'm sorry I interrupted," she murmured, turning to leave. "We can talk later."

"Devon, wait, I didn't mean to snap at you," he called after her, hurrying around the desk to catch her hand in his as she reached the door. As his thumb began to play idly with the tips of her small, slender fingers, he smiled apologetically. "Really, you're not bothering me at all. I just have a foul temper when the paperwork piles up on me and I can't get outdoors often enough. I'm sorry I took my frustration out on you. Now, what is it you wanted to talk about?"

"It's . . . well, could we sit down?" she began hesitantly, easing her hand from his, sighing inwardly with relief as he released her. They settled themselves on a well-worn black leather sofa, and she adjusted her denim skirt.

100

"Well, Devon?" he prompted after a moment. "What is it?"

"I've been thinking about what I could do around here," she blurted out impulsively, ignoring the puzzled frown that knitted his brow. "I mean, everybody else is always so busy, but all I do is tell Emily what chores I want her to do in our rooms and I take care of Jonathan. That's all I do."

"Isn't that enough?" he asked wryly. "It seems to me that caring for a baby is a full-time job."

"But times like now—when he's sleeping—I should have something to do."

"Have you ever heard of resting? You might try that."

"I'm really serious about this, Ryan," she said soberly, determined to make him understand. "Why should I rest when everybody else stays busy all day? I . . . I feel like I'm not . . . not earning my keep."

"Earning your keep! Now, what the hell does that mean?" he asked irritably, raking his fingers through his dark hair. "I didn't bring you here to make a servant of you! In fact, one of the reasons I brought you here was to see that you got some much-needed rest!"

"But I don't need to rest!"

"Don't you, Devon?" he muttered roughly, catching her chin between his thumb and forefinger, turning her face toward the light filtering through the homespun curtains covering the window. His darkening eyes examined the delicate contours of her face. "If you don't need rest, then why do I always feel you might shatter if I touch you? Why do you look so damned breakable?"

"Oh, come on, I think I look just like I always have."

"No! No, you don't," he insisted. "You didn't look this way last year. My God, when I saw you up close in that restaurant a week ago, I was astounded and very upset."

"I'm sorry the way I look disturbs you, but this must be one of those times when appearances are deceiving, because I'm fine, Ryan. Good Lord, all I did was have a

101

baby. Other women do it all the time, most of them without falling apart."

Ryan's hands closed gently on her shoulders. "But most women don't have the difficult time you did, Devon; you have to realize that. Why else do you think Dr. Turner says you shouldn't . . ." He halted for a moment with a frustrated sigh. "Why do you think he told you to take better care of yourself, to be sure to get plenty of rest? Because you haven't regained your strength yet, that's why."

"But I feel strong enough to want to do something useful around here," she persisted stubbornly. "I don't want to be treated like some kind of invalid."

"Damn, you just never give up, do you?" he muttered disagreeably, releasing her to massage the nape of his neck. His eyes impaled hers. "All right, what is it you'd like to do? Shall I make you a cowhand or will you settle for something less strenuous?"

"Something less strenuous, please," she said, laughing softly up at him. Then her breath caught in her throat as he suddenly reached out to trace the full curve of her lips with one fingertip.

"I like to hear you laugh," he said, his eyes taking on a disturbing glimmer. "Last year when we were together, you laughed a lot, but you don't much anymore."

"I'm older now; I guess that's why," she answered flatly, then hastened back to the original subject. "I . . . I was hoping I could do something to help around the house, but Maggie has everything organized, of course, and she has Emily to help her and the cook. So . . . so I was wondering if maybe I could help with the bookkeeping. I have some experience . . ."

"An accountant in Houston keeps our books, Devon."

"Oh, I see. Then I guess I'll just have to think of something else," she said airily, trying not to show her disappointment. She had already searched her brain for something she might be able to do and helping with the

102

books had been the only feasible possibility. "Well, I'll let you get back to your work while I try to think of some other idea."

Something like indecision played on Ryan's face for a second before he caught her hands in his. "Now that I think of it, you might be a great help to me," he said, inclining his head toward his cluttered desk. "As you see, I have quite a mess on my hands. It's always that way. Needless to say, I hate paperwork, but maybe you could make it simpler for me."

"But . . . but didn't you once tell me that you like to work alone and do everything yourself?"

"Maybe I should try it with help and see how it goes that way. But you'd better remember I can be a tyrant. That's definitely a warning. Now, are you willing to experiment?"

Nothing could have pleased her more, but she tried not to appear too grateful as she nodded. "Yes, I'm willing to experiment, but how would I be able to help you?"

"I always have quite a number of business letters to answer, and I also record notes for my lectures. Do you think you could transcribe them from tapes? It helps a great deal to actually have my notes on paper, but it takes me forever to transcribe them myself." He shrugged resignedly. "I have to admit I'm not what you'd call a speedy typist."

"I can help you then," she said with obvious relief. "I'm really glad." One small hand came out tentatively. She started to touch his arm, but wary of any physical contact with him, decided against it. Instead she smiled hopefully. "And I was wondering if you'd mind my writing in here. You have all these history books about the early West I could use. You see, I've been reading your great-grand-mother's diary, and it gave me a terrific idea for a story. I'm going to fictionalize the life of a young pioneer wife. I'm really excited about it and can't wait to get started."

Ryan's previously pleasant expression vanished. Hard

blue eyes raked over her. "So that's what this is all about. You only offered to help me so I'd be in the right mood to let you write in here."

"That's not true! I—"

"You shouldn't have troubled yourself," he went on relentlessly, ignoring her protest. "By all means, work in here. Why should I care? You can write wherever you damn well please."

Resentment, never far from the surface anyhow, surged through her, then bubbled over at his disparaging tone. "I'll have you know I had no ulterior motive for offering to help you with your paperwork," she said bitterly. "I want to help. But I also want to write, and I don't appreciate your acting like that's some kind of crime. What else can I do while I'm here? I'm not like your precious Iris. I can't . . . won't spend my life on horseback!"

"You could do worse. And you usually do," Ryan retorted coldly as he strode from the study.

When the door banged shut behind him, a dragging ache in Devon's stomach accompanied a slight wobbling of her chin. With firm resolve, she held her head high, willing away the tears that threatened. So he preferred Iris to her—she had always known that. It shouldn't hurt so much to actually hear him say that he did.

Despite their argument, Devon and Ryan established a routine during the next few days, and their arrangement worked better than she had expected. She didn't always have to wait until Jonathan was sleeping to get to her work. He was often content to lie in a playpen in the study, as long as she paused occasionally to talk to him and touch him. Ryan, for his part, seemed to notice the other two only on occasion. While Jonathan wriggled and surveyed his surroundings and Devon transcribed Ryan's notes, Ryan recorded more, his melodious voice muffled as he sat with his back to the room to avoid distractions.

He *could* be a tyrant, Devon discovered after a few autocratic commands were issued to her, but she really didn't mind. At least when they worked, he treated her impersonally and she was actually able to relax, giving her tautly strung nerves a much-needed rest. And it was gratifying to finally have the time to begin the first draft of her novel.

The Monday after Devon began her duties, she and Jonathan were left alone in the study about nine thirty in the morning. Luke had come in for Ryan, saying that one of the bore pumps had shut down. Since neither he nor the mechanic were having any luck trying to repair it, he had assumed Ryan would want to come take a look. So Ryan had gone.

The study seemed empty without him, but Devon typed on. Jonathan began to fret very early, as if he too missed the sound of Ryan's voice. Switching off the electric typewriter, Devon stood to bend over the playpen and lift him out. After dancing him around the room once, she sat down on the leather sofa, holding him on her lap as she tried to keep him entertained with a few of his favorite toys.

"How about an extra walk outside today? Would you like that?" she said as he maneuvered the ear of a soft plastic teddy bear into his eagerly awaiting mouth. "We could go down to the horse paddock and maybe see that big black stallion you like to watch."

Deciding some fresh air would do them both good, she started to stand, but before she could get to her feet, the study door opened.

"Well, well, well," drawled the tall young woman who entered. "This must be my lucky day. I didn't expect to run across mother and new baby in the study of all places. Where's the proud papa?"

With Jonathan perched on her knees, Devon sat motionless, watching the girl's gleaming chestnut hair swirl around her cheeks as she tossed her head imperiously.

"I'm Iris Jenkins. Where's Ryan?" the girl added impatiently after a brief silence. Hooking her thumbs in the

105

back pockets of her jeans, she inspected Devon thoroughly from head to foot, her dark eyes narrowed. With a disparaging sniff, she ambled farther into the room. "I asked you where Ryan is."

"Oh. He's out with Luke. Something about a pump," Devon finally managed to answer evenly, meeting the other girl's steady stare. Sitting back on the sofa again with Jonathan resting on her shoulder, she was determined to maintain composure. Iris was not really the way she had expected her to be. Instead of being immaculately clad in a fancy riding habit, which undoubtedly she wore in the many horse shows she participated in, she was casually dressed, practically personifying the outdoors. Her tailored blue-and-green Western shirt and the snug jeans accentuated her boyishly slim figure and height. Posing by the desk, she leaned on one hand, crossing her booted ankles.

"Well, did Ryan happen to say when he'd be back?" she asked cattily, flicking a strand of hair back over her shoulder. "Or does he tell you that much? I bet he's never told you about me."

"He didn't have to." To veil the sadness Devon knew must show in her eyes, she glanced down at Jonathan. "I knew he was engaged to you—I saw something about it in a Dallas paper last summer. I know my presence here—and, of course, Jonathan's—has upset your own plans."

"*What?*" Iris exclaimed, her voice breaking. "My plans! You . . . you mean, Ryan told you. . . ."

"I said I read about it in a newspaper," Devon muttered dully. "What did I need to be told after that?"

"Well, I'll be damned," Iris said musingly as she stared at the younger girl. Then a certain perverse amusement lighted her eyes, and she began to laugh brittlely. "This is amazing, simply amazing. I thought Ryan was going to give you some story about a fake engagement. . . . And he did try to tell you that, didn't he? I can see it in your eyes! But you just didn't believe him."

106

"No," Devon said stiffly, resenting the laughter and feeling a violent urge to scratch the older girl's smirking face. "I didn't believe him."

"Well, our engagement *wasn't* really official," Iris said smoothly, examining her fingernails. "Not a lot of people knew about it, and the newspaper item was just a lucky guess. You see, Ryan and I just sort of reached an understanding two or three years ago; we simply knew we'd be getting married eventually."

Devon's eyes widened in dismay and her cheeks paled. "You . . . you mean, Ryan was engaged to you last year when . . . when . . ."

"When he had his little fling with you?" Iris finished for her, then shrugged carelessly. "Well, like I said, we had an understanding."

"And . . . and you could forgive him, even after you learned about Jonathan?" Devon exclaimed disbelievingly. "It didn't bother you that we'd . . . we'd . . ."

"Oh, I guess it bothered me a little," Iris admitted, without much concern. "But I do try to be modern in my attitudes. After all, Ryan is a very virile man and he was on that lecture tour for nearly two months. I should have gone with him when he asked me to; if I'd been with him, he wouldn't have had to . . . Well, you know what I mean. All his needs would have been satisfied."

Devon felt horrendously sick. The morals of these people were completely beyond her comprehension. She knew she could never reach their level of sophistication. Maybe Iris could forgive Ryan for what he had done, but she couldn't. As she swallowed convulsively, she felt a nearly overpowering need to lean her head against Jonathan and cry for him and for herself. But she couldn't do that. She knew she couldn't do it.

Iris stood watching her, lazily rocking back and forth on her heels. When Devon finally forced herself to look up again, the older girl smiled pertly and spread her hands in a resigned gesture.

107

"Oh, well, I'm glad it's all out in the open, aren't you?" she said blithely. "I do hate playing games. I told Ryan we didn't need to keep our relationship a secret from you, but he was afraid you'd keep him from seeing the baby if you knew. You know, I was surprised he was so fond of Jonathan, but now that I've seen him, I understand. He looks so much like Ryan." Suddenly, she strode over to stand before Devon, holding out her arms. "Could I hold him? Would you let me, just for a minute?"

Devon's arms tightened around her son as she shook her head emphatically. "No, he cries when strangers hold him," she lied. "Maybe you should wait until he knows you better."

Iris snapped her fingers jauntily as she lowered her arms again. "Okay, I'll wait. I'm sure Jonny and I will be great friends soon. And . . ." Her expression sobered abruptly. "And I do hope we can be friends, too, Devon. We're both civilized human beings, and we both understand this situation, so let's try to be friends for Ryan's sake, okay?"

Before Devon could recover her composure sufficiently to speak, Ryan walked into the study. He halted midstride, displeasure tightening his jaw. With a murmur of welcome, Iris ran to him, pressing a reluctantly restrained kiss against his cheek.

Though he tried to be discreet and stepped away from the other girl, the action was too little and too late to ease any of Devon's pain. She looked away, gathering Jonathan closer against her as a hard, aching knot tightened in her chest. And Iris wanted them to be friends, she thought, anguish tearing at her. Well, maybe the older girl was confident enough to be generous, but Devon was the big loser in this ridiculously tangled mess and becoming Iris's friend was far beyond her unsophisticated capabilities. She knew she could never, ever be that noble.

To hang onto her sanity and to ease some of the humiliation she felt, Devon began to defy Ryan at every opportunity. If he told her she was working in the study too much, she arranged it so she worked even longer. If he asked her to go along when he took Jonathan out for a walk, she always fabricated some excuse. Such small attempts at rebellion gave her little satisfaction, but they were the only defense she had and the only way she could retaliate for what he had done. And whenever he became impatient with the way she was acting, she was innocence itself, pretending she had no idea she was doing anything that might irritate him. To save her own life, she wouldn't have told him how devastating her conversation with Iris had been. If he wasn't sensitive enough to realize how she must be feeling, then she certainly wasn't going to enlighten him. She had some pride left, though she really didn't know how.

It was a miserable time. All the tension had come back between them, following them even into the study. Ryan cursed frequently as he rifled through the papers on his desk, and Devon made so many mistakes in her typing that she sometimes ached to pound the electric typewriter to a pulp with a sledgehammer. Even Jonathan got in on the act, probably sensing their moods. As soon as Devon sat down at the typewriter, he invariably began to fret and whine until she could have screamed.

She felt so horribly alone and angry and hurt. Now she would have welcomed going to Corpus Christi, even to live permanently. She would have gone anywhere to escape the pain she felt in this house and to escape the ever-present fear that Iris would come ambling in at any given moment. *Iris.* Devon loathed her and loathed herself for feeling that way.

Mercifully, Iris stayed away for over a week after her first visit, but she would come back. Devon knew she would and that knowledge kept her on edge every minute of every day. It did nothing for her ego to realize Iris obviously didn't feel at all threatened by her. Devon knew if she had been in the older girl's position, she would have been climbing the walls at the thought of Ryan sharing a

109

house with another woman, especially a woman who had borne him a child. Yet Iris had seemed to adjust to the situation with amazing speed and apparently had no doubts that she and Ryan would begin their life together as soon as he fulfilled his self-imposed obligation to his son. Iris's supreme confidence made Devon feel totally inconsequential, almost nonexistent. She had no desire even to see the older girl, much less become bosom buddies with her.

Unfortunately, Iris had other ideas. She arrived at the ranch Thursday morning, over a week after her first visit and two days before Maggie's annual summer party. Dragging two large suitcases with her as if she meant to stay at least a month, she claimed she had come only to help Maggie with preparations for the party. Maggie welcomed her with open arms, making Devon feel even more *de trop.* She liked Ryan's stepmother, and though Maggie was always nice to her, it was obvious that she loved Iris as if she were a daughter.

Devon's spirits dropped to an all-time low. Though Iris had said she had come to help Maggie, she spent most of her time cornering Devon alone. Even Devon's unenthusiastic response to her friendly overtures did not deter her. Devon decided Iris was either the most insensitive human being in the world or the most simple-minded. She had to be one or the other or perhaps both. No normal young woman would try to befriend the girl who had borne her fiancé's baby.

While Jonathan slept that Friday afternoon, Devon hid herself in her room, though she did not really expect Iris to come badgering her anytime soon. Immediately after lunch, Ryan had left the house. Since Iris had soon followed Devon was sure they were planning to meet somewhere. It was the third time since Thursday morning that they had managed to disappear at the same time. As far as Devon was concerned, that was two times too many to possibly be coincidence.

Flinging herself face down on her bed, she clenched and unclenched her small fists against the snowy white chenille bedspread. At that moment, she could have murdered both Ryan and Iris, unmindful of the consequences, and would have thoroughly enjoyed doing it. They were both despicable and not very bright if they believed she didn't know they were meeting each other every chance they got.

Where did they go? she wondered bleakly, turning over to stare blindly at the ceiling. It didn't take any great imagination to guess *what* they did together, but she had no idea where they went to find the privacy they needed. Yet, maybe it was best for her not to know where they went. Already, she could close her eyes and see them together, kissing, making love. If she knew exactly where they went for their trysts, the haunting images would become only that much clearer. She groaned softly as an agonizing jealousy ripped through her. If only Ryan hadn't seen her that day in the restaurant. If only she and Jonathan were back in Boston again, living the way they had before, dull as that life had been. There was something to be said for dullness. Right now she would have gladly exchanged the sharp stabbing in her chest for the numbness that came when every day was the same as the one before.

Refusing to release the sob that suddenly rose in her throat, Devon curled up on the bed, hugging her knees against her, wishing with all her heart she could fall asleep. But she couldn't. Her nerves were so on edge that she felt she would scream if she didn't do something soon to relieve some of her tension. Suddenly, she swung her feet off the bed, jumped up, and hurriedly changed to her navy maillot swimsuit.

Outside, the blazing sun beat down on Devon's bare head. Not wasting a moment, she rushed across the terrace and dived with neat precision into the pool. Sparkling water enclosed her, cooling her heated skin. She surfaced, and after swimming the length of the pool twice, some of

111

the tension she had previously felt began to ease. Turning onto her back, she floated, her eyes tightly closed to the sun's glare. She managed to thrust her suspicions about Iris and Ryan to the back of her mind and simply enjoyed the silken texture of the water that caressed her skin.

About five minutes later, an eerie sensation that she was being watched made her tense. An instant before she sank ignominiously beneath the surface, her eyes opened slightly. Ryan was standing by the edge of the pool. Instinct had caused her to take a deep breath before she had gone under, and now she swam half the pool's length underwater. But all the fun was gone. Hoping Ryan would go away if she pretended she hadn't noticed him, she spent the next couple minutes paddling idly on the far side of the pool, taking care not even to glance in his direction.

Her ploy didn't succeed. He didn't leave. Instead, he suddenly appeared in front of her, going down on his heels on the tiled apron. She was holding onto the edge and lazily kicking her feet out behind her. Devon had no choice except to acknowledge his presence. With a curt nod, she took in the tousled disorder of his dark hair and tried to ignore the keen shaft of pain she felt when she noticed a trace of lipstick on his khaki shirt collar. It was so obvious that he had been with Iris that Devon didn't trust herself even to speak to him. Terrified she might burst into tears, she swam with quick, jerky strokes to the tiled steps at the end of the pool.

Ryan followed. When she emerged from the water, crystalline droplets shimmering on her satiny skin, he allowed his narrowed gaze to rove slowly over her. Then he smiled slightly. "Enjoying yourself?"

"Not nearly as much as you've been, I'm sure," she retorted almost inaudibly.

Unfortunately, he heard what she said. When she tried to sweep past him, he reached out and caught one delicate wrist in his hand. "What exactly did that remark mean?"

His seemingly puzzled tone didn't impress her in the

least. Tilting her head back, she glared up at him. "I don't see any need to elaborate. I'm sure you know exactly what I meant."

"If I knew, I wouldn't have asked for an explanation, would I?"

"Oh, for heaven's sake, Ryan, don't try to play games with me!" Devon demanded resentfully. "I don't appreciate it one bit."

"What the devil . . ." He broke off with an exasperated sigh. Shaking his head, he gripped her shoulders in large hands and gazed intently into her eyes. "Devon, I'm not trying to play games with you. For God's sake, I don't even know what you're talking about."

Though she had realized long ago that he was an accomplished actor, this particular performance was right up there in the award-winning category. If Devon hadn't known him better, she might have believed that he truly was confused. But she did know him and was in no mood to be his gullible little patsy again. Flexing her shoulders impatiently, she tried once more to move away from him. When his fingers pressed harder into her flesh, she snapped at him, "Do you *mind*? I want to go inside. It's hot out here, and besides, Jonathan might wake up from his nap."

"If he does, Maggie will gladly look after him," Ryan answered, deftly reclaiming the advantage by the simple method of speaking calmly.

"Well, I want to go in anyway. So let me go," Devon demanded hotly in contrast. His hands on her merely served to remind her that he had undoubtedly just left a romantic encounter with his beloved Iris. When he reached up to take a wispy strand of her drying hair between his fingers and his knuckles grazed the curve of her cheek, she could tolerate his touch no longer. "Let go!" she reiterated huskily. A knot of unshed tears constricted her throat. In desperation, she grasped his wrists to try to push his hands away from her.

113

"Devon, what's wrong?" he muttered roughly. With incredible ease he freed himself from her grip and feathered his fingers down her bare arms. His bronze skin was still amazingly dark in comparison to the light tan she had acquired since she'd been at the ranch. Hard yet gentle hands curved into the enticing insweep of her waist. He drew her a step closer. His piercing eyes searched her face. "You haven't said a civil word to me in days. And despite the sun you've been getting, you still look too pale. So unhappy. I wish you'd tell me what's the matter."

"Nothing's the matter," she lied defiantly. She wasn't about to tell him she probably was pale because the thought of him and Iris together had made her feel almost physically ill today. Instead, she handed him that old, standard excuse, "I just haven't been feeling very well."

"Oh, God, you're not pregnant again, are you?" he exclaimed roughly, visibly upset. A muscle moved convulsively in his clenched jaw and what seemed to be a combination of anguish and shame darkened his eyes. He shook her slightly. "Tell me, Devon. Could you possibly be pregnant again?"

"I didn't say that. I only said I hadn't been feeling well," she countered lazily, finding some perverse comfort in his anxiety. "You're just ridiculously obsessed with the fear that I might be pregnant again and I don't know why. I've told you I wouldn't expect anything from you if I were. I assure you I can easily take care of everything myself."

With frightening speed, his anxiety became anger. "What do you mean you can take care of everything yourself?" he growled. "That sounds very much like you're considering an abortion. If you are, put the thought right out of your mind. I'll be watching you. You'll never be able to get to a doctor without my knowing it. I guess maybe I'm just lucky you didn't abort Jonathan early in that pregnancy. Why didn't you? Didn't you realize you were pregnant early enough to get rid of him?"

114

Devon blanched. A thousand memories assailed her, memories of extreme bouts of morning sickness that extended far into the day, and memories of the long, difficult delivery she had endured alone. And she had gone through all of it because she ached to hold Ryan's child in her arms. Now he dared to stand there and hurl nasty, obscene accusations at her, actually insinuate she had never wanted Jonathan. She couldn't stand still and listen to it. Pride lifted her small chin. In silence, she tried to sidestep him, but he caught her wrist and pulled her toward him to firmly grip her waist.

So close against him now that she had to lean back to see his face, she stared at him, green eyes bright with anger and a trace of tears. "I never expected you to be that cruel and unfair," she said stiffly. "Remarks like that can almost make me hate you."

"I thought you already did," he muttered. One large hand slipped from her waist and long, lean fingers spread open across her flat abdomen. "You certainly don't have to tell me you're not overly fond of me. Your attitude does that. But, for God's sake, Devon, please tell me whether or not you're pregnant again."

His hand scorched her skin through the damp swimsuit. Devon recoiled and pushed his arm away. "No, I'm not pregnant. I'm *absolutely* sure I'm not going to have another baby. Does that make you happy? Does it relieve you to know you won't be tied to me any more than you already are? I do hope so. And let me tell you something else, Ryan. I had Jonathan because I *wanted* him. Wanted him in spite of everything. I could have had an abortion, but I didn't. How could you possibly know how I felt then? You were nowhere around, so don't accuse me. . . . Oh, Ryan, that was a horrid thing to say!"

Regarding her intently, he finally sighed and touched her hair again. "You're right. I shouldn't have said that. I didn't mean it. I'm sorry, but, my God, Devon, sometimes you just frustrate me so much that I lash out at you.

Lately, you've been particularly difficult. I've wanted to talk to you again about us getting married, but I knew you probably wouldn't listen to what I had to say."

"I don't think there's anything to say," she answered huskily. "I can't imagine why you'd even consider marrying a woman you mistrust as much as you mistrust me. You even believe I'd rather have not had Jonathan."

"I just told you I didn't mean that."

"But you said it, Ryan, so maybe you do believe it just a little," she said softly, accusingly. When he started to protest again, the sudden stubborn set of her jaw apparently silenced him. With one last compulsive glance at the lipstick on his collar, she turned away and hurried back to the house.

Saturday night, Devon stood at her window gazing out. The full, cream-colored moon rose into the inky sky above a line of white stratus clouds edging the far horizon. Off in the distance, a coyote mournfully howled, contributing yet another lonely sound to the wind whispering in the high branches of the cottonwoods around the ranch house.

Devon couldn't deny that there was true beauty in the land, but it was a beauty that saddened her rather than gave her joy. Beauty sometimes needed to be shared, and there was no one on the ranch with whom she could share it. Jonathan was a trifle young to appreciate the aesthetic wonder of a moonrise. If it didn't look like something he could put into his mouth, he usually wasn't very interested.

With a rueful smile, Devon turned from the window, catching sight of her reflection in the full-length mirror across the room. Though her hair, pulled back from her temples in loose, silvery sweeps and clasped in black-enamel barrettes, looked nice enough, she couldn't exactly say the same for the clothes she had chosen to wear. Her black taffeta skirt wasn't in the latest style and her white silk blouse was also slightly dated. It was unfortunate that both garments were a tad too large for her, but she supposed she looked fairly presentable. Fluffing the frothy cravat of lace that nestled against her creamy throat, she gazed speculatively at her reflection, then glanced at her wristwatch.

Seven thirty. She'd better not dawdle any longer or Maggie would come drag her out to the party. She didn't want to go. The evening promised to be difficult to endure. People from the neighboring ranches and others from as far away as Dallas had arrived for the party and the barbecue the next day. Devon didn't know a single one of them. And she was afraid that most of them would have heard about her—the interloper who had wrecked Ryan and Iris's wedding plans.

No, it definitely wasn't going to be easy to face all the curious glances, yet there was no avoiding the inevitable. She could hardly refuse to make an appearance. That would really start tongues wagging. With a sigh, she freshened the rose-tinted gloss on her lips, then drew herself up to her full height and proceeded out of her room into the hall.

She had gone no more than a few steps when she heard Ryan's door open. Stopping, she half turned and attempted a smile. That failed miserably as his eyes darted over her and a deep frown etched itself into his tan brow. With one long stride, he was near enough to reach out and grip her arm roughly, impelling her back into her room. He slammed the door behind them. "Why the hell are you wearing those clothes?" he exclaimed impatiently. "You should have packed up all your old things and sent them into town for the annual church charity rummage sale." He lifted a silencing hand when she tried to speak. "Oh, no, don't try to tell me you didn't have anything to wear, because I know better, remember."

"I remember," she muttered, her eyes clouding with resentment. "You tried to soothe your conscience by buy-

117

ing out a dress shop. But I'm not that easily bought, I'll have you know, so tonight I'll wear clothes I paid for myself, if you don't mind."

"Hell, yes, I mind!" he retorted harshly, taking a step toward her. "I mind your walking out there looking like an orphan in clothes that don't really fit you. And I mind the way you've been acting lately, like a schoolgirl trying to assert her independence by rebelling at anything and everything! Where did you learn such nonsense? Did you just decide to disagree with everything because that would make you seem tough? If you did, you were wrong. It just makes you look silly. And I'm damned well tired of you acting that way!"

"Well, that's just too bad, isn't it?" she snapped back recklessly, glaring up at him. "I'm damned well tired of the way you act too, so we're even. And you're wasting your time if you think I'm going to change clothes now. Either I wear what I have on or I don't leave this room."

"Don't bet on that, little girl," he warned ominously, stalking to her closet to pull out the simply styled, long, white crocheted dress he'd insisted she buy in town. "Here, put it on," he commanded, tossing the dress at her. "And be damned quick about it!"

Refusing to be intimidated, Devon placed her hands on her hips, shaking her head as she muttered, "No way."

"Oh, Devon, be careful," he said, his voice deceptively soft as he moved close enough to tower above her. "I have no idea what's been making you act like a little idiot lately. Maybe it's be-obstinate-and-drive-someone-crazy month, I don't know. But whatever it is, I've had enough of it. Now put on that dress."

"This dress?" she countered sarcastically, holding up the white crochet. "But won't all your guests have a good laugh if I show up wearing such a virginal little thing. I'm sure they all know we have a son although we never bothered to get married."

118

"Not because of a lack of willingness on my part! I've asked you often enough to marry me."

"Let's not start that discussion again," she said sharply. "And I won't wear that dress. It's too innocent looking, and motherhood and innocence don't really go together."

For a moment, Ryan's penetrating gaze swept over her, then he murmured, "You really think becoming a mother changed the way you looked? It didn't. As small as you are and with that cloud of silver hair so soft around your face, you look like a little girl, like no man could have ever touched you. Sometimes I can hardly believe I made love to you myself, much less that Andrews . . ."

"Don't, Ryan, don't," she pleaded, far too disturbed by his words and the sudden gentling of his tone.

"Put the dress on," he whispered coaxingly. "Please."

She shook her head, unable to let him always win so easily.

"Then I'll put it on you myself," he cautioned softly, reaching out to loosen the lace cravat at her throat.

As he deftly unfastened the first two buttons of her blouse and his rough fingertips brushed her skin, her pent-up resentment and pain burst forth in a fury. "Damn you! Oh, *damn* you!" she cried when she was unable to dislodge his fingers. Beyond rational thought, she pressed her palms against his broad, muscular chest, shoving at him with all her strength. It wasn't enough. When his arm clamped around her waist, dragging her against him, she strained away, twisting her body in a futile attempt to escape. Her fingernails bit into his shoulders through the thickness of the cream-colored turtleneck he wore.

Her resistance did not deter him at all. With a muffled curse, he pinned her arms behind her back, holding both her wrists in one hand as he undid the remaining buttons of her blouse with the other.

"You . . . *you!*" she gasped, twisting in his hard grip as he slipped the blouse off her shoulders, then unfastened her skirt so that it fell to the floor in a heap.

119

"Little hellcat," he muttered, breathing raggedly. His narrowed eyes lazily surveyed the shapely length of leg exposed by the slit in her long half slip. Then his disturbing gaze moved up to linger on the rapid rise and fall of breasts covered by a diaphanous lace bra. His fingertips were suddenly trailing over the firm mounds, lightly tracing the darker peaks discernible through the sheer white lace. When the aroused nipples swelled to his probing touch, he smiled and whispered seductively, "But what a desirable little hellcat. I'm taking you to bed. That's exactly what you need."

"I . . . I don't need anything from *you*," she whispered back breathlessly. "So this time, you'll have to . . . force me."

"I'd be delighted," he muttered, sweeping her up into his arms to carry her to the bed. Even as her head touched the pillow, he was beside her, pinning her legs beneath the sinewy length of one of his. Yet his mouth teasingly brushing her lips possessed an unnerving gentleness.

Devon held herself stiff and unyielding beneath him, refusing to respond to the enveloping warmth emanating from his body. But as his teeth closed on her lower lip, tugging her mouth open slightly, a quickening ache uncurled inside her and radiated down to weaken her thighs.

"No!" she gasped, trying to turn her head to escape the persuasive pressure of his hard, seeking mouth. "Ryan, *please.*"

Strong fingers tangled in the silkiness of her hair. He held her face fast between his palms and kissed her relentlessly, ravishing the soft sweetness of her lips.

Devon's clenched fists opened slowly, her fingers beginning to trace the outline of the taut muscles of his chest. Suddenly she was clinging to him, wrapping her slender arms around his neck.

"You drive me crazy," he groaned, his hands roaming over her, cupping and caressing her breasts and massaging her thighs. He slid his hands beneath her hips, arching her against the thrusting aggression of his hard, angular body. "God, I *need* you, Devon. I need to spend long nights in this bed with you."

Somehow, Devon dragged herself back to reality. He had said he *needed* her, not that he loved her. At least that first time, he had uttered the lie, making surrender irresistible. This time she had to resist; love was what she wanted from him. Mere physical need would never be enough. She had learned that much that night in Corpus Christi.

"No, Ryan, no," she whispered, tensing beneath him. "I . . . I can't."

"Yes, you can," he whispered back against her parted lips. "You need me, too. I know you do."

"No, Ryan!"

When she pushed at him, he pinned her hands back beside her head, lifting his mouth from hers.

"Don't play games," he warned hoarsely. "Don't fight me, Devon, I don't want to hurt you."

A primitive fear of what he might do pulsated through her. A soft sob escaped her lips when someone mercifully knocked on the door.

"Devon, come along soon, dear," Maggie called from the hallway. "Everyone's so anxious to meet you."

"Damn them all!" Ryan groaned, dragging his hands reluctantly from around Devon's waist. He sat up on the edge of the bed, raking his fingers through his hair. Glinting sapphire eyes held her gaze. "Later," he whispered. "We'll finish this later."

"We're finished now," she answered dully, closing her eyes on the passion in his. "I know how you'd hate to risk making me pregnant again, so I guess you'd better just let Iris go on satisfying *all* your sexual needs."

"Stretching a bit far for a rationalization, aren't you?" he muttered cryptically. He got to his feet and thrust his hands deep into the pockets of his black trousers. He glanced back over his shoulder and said mockingly as she opened her eyes again, "Better shore up your defenses,

121

little Devon. Remember, Maggie's giving my room to some of the guests who'll stay over tonight. So I've decided to sleep in here with you. Maybe we *will* finish what we started."

Refusing to dignify his remark with a response, she sat up. Swinging her feet off the bed, she smoothed her tousled hair with trembling hands.

"M . . . Maggie's waiting," she said. "I'd better get dressed."

"I'll wait in the hall for you," he announced grimly as he strode to the door. "And wear what you damned well please. Pity you don't have a hair shirt—then you could really play the martyr; heaven knows, you seem to enjoy the role."

After he had opened the door and stepped out, Devon stood on unsteady legs, pressing her fingers against the throbbing in her temples. He was right about one thing. Defying him about clothes and other trivial matters was foolish indeed, a desperate adolescent hoax she had perpetrated on herself to make her believe she still controlled her own existence. She didn't, though. Ryan controlled everything, even her body's responses. Dragging around in shoddy old clothes wasn't going to change anything.

With a tremulous sigh, Devon picked up the crocheted dress that had fallen to the floor during their little tussle. She put it on. After running a brush through her hair, she caught sight of her reflection in the mirror. At least she looked nice, she thought bleakly as she opened her bedroom door.

Five hours later, Devon was back in her room, waiting for Ryan to return with Jonathan, who had been in the care of Luke's wife during the party. She sat down on the edge of the bed, too tired at the moment to worry about Ryan sharing her room for the night. She could worry about that later. Slipping her shoes off, she wriggled her toes in the soft nap of the carpet and smiled slightly.

Surprisingly, she had actually enjoyed the party. All Maggie's guests had been nice to her, exhibiting their genuine Texas friendliness. She relaxed and participated fully in some very interesting conversations. And, to her knowledge, no one had snickered behind her back, despite her virginal attire. Everyone had shown her the utmost respect. She could only hope it wasn't solely because Ryan had stayed by her side nearly every moment, convincingly playing the role of the happy, attentive fiancé. Even Iris, tactless as she sometimes was, had been discreet enough not to seek Ryan out and draw attention to the ridiculous triangle the three of them comprised. Yet, the evening had been exhausting all the same. Devon heaved a sigh of relief when she finally heard Ryan open the door to the nursery.

"Did he wake up?" she asked after hurrying to Jonathan's room.

"He's out like a light," Ryan whispered, taking her arm to guide her back into her own room. "And I tucked him in snugly; don't worry."

Easing her arm free, she murmured her thanks.

"Think nothing of it," he said flatly. "Now, if you'll give me a couple blankets, I can make a place to sleep on the floor."

"You don't have to do that," she said weakly after only a moment's hesitation. "Th . . . the bed's very big. Big enough for both of us to sleep without . . . without . . ."

"Without ever touching each other," he finished mockingly, then shrugged. "Fine with me. But are you sure you can trust me?"

Though she nodded, she was wondering a few minutes later if she had made a mistake. Had her offer to share the bed seemed like an invitation? Her heart thudding, she turned out the lamp, shed her robe in the darkness, then climbed in beneath the sheet with Ryan. She turned over onto her side, clinging as close to the edge of the bed as possible, scarcely able to breathe. She lay there for a long time, tensed and waiting, expecting Ryan's hand to descend on her shoulder and turn her to him. But he made no move to touch her, and finally, exhausted, she fell asleep.

CHAPTER SEVEN

Feeling positively inspired, Devon progressed rapidly on the early chapters of the first draft of her novel. Ryan's great-grandmother's diary fired her imagination, and to her delight she found she could easily identify with Louisa Wilder. In 1873, at age nineteen, the new bride of Jacob Wilder had come to the Texas plains feeling as much uncertainty as Devon herself had felt only weeks ago. Drawing on the entries in Louisa's diary and on her own emotions, Devon was able to create a truly believable heroine. She quickly became immersed in her story. Everything around her ceased to exist when she wrote. Only Ryan, Jonathan, or Maggie could risk interrupting her without evoking obvious impatience. All other potential intruders were politely discouraged.

Unfortunately, Iris Jenkins was never one to be discouraged, politely or otherwise. On a Friday afternoon, while Devon concentrated on proofreading a paragraph she had just written, the older woman ambled into the study. Seemingly unaware of Devon's sudden disgruntled grimace, she nonchalantly fanned her flushed cheeks, then unfastened the second button of her faded Western shirt.

"My, riding in that sun is mighty hot today, even if this is supposed to be a cooler spell," she drawled, dropping down onto the leather sofa to smile too sweetly at Devon. "You ride once in a while, don't you. Been out today?"

Shaking her head, Devon tried to smile with some semblance of cordiality. Since Iris hadn't been pestering her as much lately, she supposed the least she could do was to appear friendly. "No, I don't ride every day. Sometimes, I'm just too busy to get away."

"Oh, yes, that's right. Ryan told me you had some idea about writing a historical novel about the Old West." Iris smiled rather smugly. "I was surprised. I mean, how can you write about this place when you hardly know which end of a horse is which?"

"I'm not quite that ignorant," Devon answered calmly despite the insulting tone. "Besides, most writers have to do a great deal of research, even about a place they're very familiar with. It's wiser; that way you're sure you've got all the facts right. And it's really rather fun. I'm learning so much about Texas and the pioneer days that I'd never known before."

"Sounds plenty dull to me. I wouldn't be the least bit interested in sitting down and trying to make up a story about what might have happened a hundred years ago. I'd rather live in the present. And I'd never be able to sit still that long, anyhow. It's much more fun to be out riding." Iris stretched her long legs out before her, flicking an imaginary piece of dust from her snug jeans. For a moment, she stared somewhat pensively at the floor. When she looked up at Devon again, her expression was unusually serious. "I guess Jonathan's asleep, isn't he?" she asked almost wistfully. "I was sort of hoping he'd be in here with you so I could play with him."

"Sorry, he's napping," Devon said, trying not to sound too relieved as she glanced back down at the sheet of paper she held. For some reason, the increasing interest Iris had in Jonathan made her feel dreadfully uneasy. Perhaps it was simple jealousy. Iris already had Ryan, and Devon didn't particularly want her to try to win some of Jonathan's affection too. Yet, simply for Jonathan's sake, she supposed she shouldn't be so petty. Iris would be his stepmother someday, and it would be better for everyone concerned if the two of them had a good, friendly relationship. Unfortunately, knowing how she should feel did not alter the way she actually felt. Jonathan was her son and she didn't want to share his love with Iris. It didn't seem quite fair somehow that she might have to someday. But that was a worry she could put aside until later. At least, she thought it was until Iris spoke again.

"You know, I really love that little boy," she said softly. "Maybe it's because he's Ryan's son, but, still, I've always been crazy about children, anyway."

"Really," Devon murmured politely. She wasn't eager to discuss maternal yearnings, especially with this girl. A mental picture of Ryan's future family was the last thing she needed at the moment. Hoping to steer the conversation to a less disturbing subject, she said, "Ryan mentioned that you worked as a teacher's assistant for a couple of years. Why did you quit? Didn't you like it?"

"Oh, it was okay. Working with children can be rewarding, but I was in Dallas and Ryan was here," Iris explained, abstracted. Then with an unusually humble expression on her face, she leaned forward, clasping her hands around her knees. "Devon, would you let . . . I mean, could I possibly take Jonathan out tomorrow morning?"

"Out? Out where?"

"Out riding."

"You mean horseback riding?" Devon exclaimed incredulously. "But, Iris, he can't even sit alone yet. I know children start learning to ride very early in Texas, but not when they're barely five months old, surely."

Iris giggled nervously. "Of course not. I didn't mean I wanted to try to put that baby on a horse. I just wanted him to ride with me."

"I don't think you realize how wriggly Jonathan can be," Devon stated, striving to be patient. "I'd never try to control him and a horse at the same time."

"Then I could put him in that canvas back carrier you

have for him," the older girl persisted eagerly. "Then he'd be all snug and safe."

"And jostled," Devon added curtly with a disgruntled wave of her hand. "No, I'm afraid the carrier wouldn't help much if Jonathan couldn't hold himself steady in it. He's not quite that coordinated yet."

Bending her head to stare at the floor, Iris muttered, "Oh, I see."

Devon stared at her, irritated that she was acting unreasonably disappointed. Not knowing what to say next, she shifted uncomfortably on her swivel chair, wishing Iris would just go away.

Iris, however, suddenly began to cry softly. "Oh, Devon, you just don't know how lucky you are," she said, tears flowing. "You just don't know."

"I can't imagine why you'd say that," Devon answered stiffly, wondering what the devil was going on. "What makes me so lucky?"

"Jonathan, of course." Iris sobbed. "You gave Ryan a child, and I envy you. I . . . I'd do anything if I could have Ryan's baby."

And I'd do anything to get you to leave me alone, Devon longed to retort. Instead, however, she began to straighten the papers on her desk, thoroughly disgusted by this latest example of Iris's insensitivity. The girl obviously had no sense. She had to be some kind of twerp to come in and tell her, of all people, that she couldn't wait to start having Ryan's babies.

Suddenly Devon felt an overwhelming need for fresh air. Muttering beneath her breath, she covered the typewriter, then stood without so much as a glance in Iris's direction.

"I'm going out for a walk. So, if you'll excuse . . ."

"I can't have children, you know," Iris interrupted abruptly with louder, renewed sobs. "I was in an automobile accident four years ago and the doctor . . . the doctor said I'd never be able to have a baby. Oh, I thought I'd

die when he told me that. You can't imagine how I
. . ."

Devon hardly heard the rest. Clutching the edge of the
desk, unaware of the sharp corner digging into her palm,
she tried to catch her breath. Heat suffused her entire
body, then drained away to leave her icy cold and shiver-
ing.

"Does . . . does Ryan know you can't have children?"
she finally asked stiffly. "Did you tell him?"

Sniffling, Iris whispered, "Of course, I told him. He had
every right to know. H . . . he was very disappointed, I
could tell, even though he tried not to show it. Oh! I can't
talk about it anymore!" Leaping to her feet, Iris made a
mad dash for the study door. Then she was gone without
another word.

"Oh my God!" Devon whispered, her cheeks white as
she sank weakly back down on her chair. Despite her
dislike for Iris, she did feel suddenly sorry for the other
woman. The unhappy circumstances of her pregnancy
with Jonathan aside, Devon still had known the joy of
bearing a child fathered by the man she loved, a joy that
Iris would never know. But Devon was afraid to think any
further, to let herself wonder what Iris's revelation could
mean.

By Thursday night, Devon was nearly in a panic. After
feeding Jonathan and tucking him into bed at ten o'clock,
she went to take a long, hot bath, but even that did nothing
to soothe her frazzled nerves. As she pulled her long,
white, cotton nightgown over her head, one of the tiny
buttons on the yoke snagged a strand of her hair. Her
hands were trembling so violently that it seemed to take
her forever to free herself. Finally, she managed. As the
narrow straps of the gown settled onto her shoulders, she
let her arms drop weakly by her sides.

She was so incredibly tired. Since her talk with Iris
yesterday afternoon, she had not known a moment's

peace. There had been no sleep for her last night. Countless theories concerning Ryan's behavior darted to and fro in her brain until she thought her head would explode. And now, after all those hours of agonizing worry, she was finally forced to accept the very real possibility that Ryan wanted to take Jonathan away from her. It made sense. He wanted Iris to be his wife, but Iris could never have his children. Devon, however, had conveniently provided him with a son, the only child he might ever father. It was logical to assume he would want to keep that child with him.

Barefoot, Devon paced the gleaming hardwood floor of her bedroom, wondering exactly what Ryan meant to do. Had he coerced her into coming to Texas where it might be easier for him to win custody of Jonathan? And was that why he had insisted she sign that affidavit acknowledging him as Jonathan's natural father? Oh, what a stupid fool she had been to sign it!

"Idiot!" she whispered as she paced. "You may have jumped right into a trap."

Could Ryan possibly be that cruel? He would have to be completely ruthless to methodically plan to take her child. Somehow, she just couldn't believe he was that ruthless. But what did she know? She hadn't imagined he would make love to her, then desert her, but he had. So maybe she simply couldn't judge him objectively. Her emotions did tend to overwhelm reason where he was concerned.

Halting midstride, she pressed her fist against the painful, tightening knot in her stomach. If he really meant to take Jonathan, could she bear the pain of knowing he didn't care how much he hurt her? She needed to believe he at least felt some compassion for her, but if he actually tried to take her baby . . .

"If, if, if," she whispered despairingly, plowing both hands through her hair. She had to stop trying to second-guess him. Instead, she must start planning how she could fight him if indeed he did try to gain exclusive custody. Yet, what *could* she do? she asked herself bleakly. She knew no one here; he probably knew some very influential people. She had no money for a lawyer, while he could afford to obtain the very best legal assistance.

"Oh, God, I probably wouldn't have a chance of winning," she muttered, the knot in her stomach beginning to make her nauseated. After turning out the lamp, she got into bed, hoping she would be able to escape her fears for at least a few hours. But simply being exhausted did not mean she could go to sleep.

Over an hour later, she sat up straight in bed, unable to suppress a soft sob of frustration as she switched on the lamp. Peering at the small clock on the table, she saw it was already twelve thirty. All her fears were still crowding her mind as relentlessly as before she had gone to bed.

She couldn't go on this way much longer without screaming. Knowing she had to get some sleep, she threw back the sheet, got out of bed, and hurried to the door. As quietly as possible, she tiptoed down the hall to the bathroom she and Ryan shared.

A minute later, she was back in her room, setting the glass of water she had gotten down on the bedside table. Still on tiptoe, she went to take her small traveling case off the shelf in her closet. She breathed a grateful sigh when she opened it. The small bottle filled with sleeping pills was nestled in one corner.

"Thank God," she murmured, snatching up the bottle and unscrewing the cap. Too many dull blue pills spilled out into her hand when she tapped the bottle. She stared at them for a moment with something like longing in her eyes. If she took them all . . . "Fool!" She scooped all but two of the tablets back into their container. She put the bottle down on the table and picked up the glass of water. Just as she started to put the pills in her mouth, her bedroom door swung open. Her hand froze in midair.

"What's the matter, Devon?" Ryan asked, thrusting his

hands into the pockets of his navy-blue terry robe. As his eyes shifted from the glass in her hand to the bottle that sat on the table, he scowled. "What are you taking?"

"My vitamins," she lied stupidly, knowing even as she uttered the words how ridiculous they sounded. Dropping the hand that held the pills, she tried to smile. "I . . . I forgot to take them this morning."

"Vitamins?" Shaking his head doubtingly, Ryan closed the door behind him and walked across the room toward her. "You got out of bed at nearly one in the morning to take vitamins? Come on now, Devon, what are you really taking?"

"Something for my headache, that's all," she murmured uncomfortably, easing her hand behind her back. "I . . . I got up to take something for my head, then . . . then I remembered I hadn't taken my vitamins."

Ryan eyed the bottle on the table with obvious suspicion. "You have such severe headaches that you need a prescription drug to ease them?"

"Well . . . well, I . . ."

"Let me see them," he commanded, holding out his hand. When she shook her head, he stepped closer. "*Devon.*" When she still made no move to obey him, he reached past her to pick up the bottle. He frowned when he saw the label. "Sedatives. These things can be dangerous, even when prescribed by a doctor," he declared, pocketing the bottle and gripping her upper arms tightly. "I really don't like the idea of your taking them, so give me the one you have in your hand."

"I don't have any," she bluffed very badly, then tried to jerk away as he grasped her arm and pulled it back around in front of her. "No! Ryan, oh, please don't take those too," she begged softly as he pried open her clenched fingers.

Relentlessly, he took both tablets from her palm and dropped them into his pocket with the bottle.

"You don't need them, Devon. You shouldn't need them."

"But I do, Ryan; I do need them," she muttered thickly, her chin wobbling as she dropped down on the easy chair beside the table. Turning, she drew her legs up beside her and pressed her face into the soft upholstered back of the chair. "Oh, God, I can't stand it," she whispered urgently, horrified at the prospect of spending another tormented night. "I just want to go to sleep; that's all I want."

"Devon, are you really that miserable here?" he exclaimed softly, resting one large hand heavily on her shoulder. "Are you?"

"I'm so tired, Ryan, just so tired," she answered weakly. "But I can't go to sleep."

When a shuddering sob shook her body, he uttered a muffled oath. He lifted her up into his arms as if she weighed no more than Jonathan and sat down in the chair himself, cradling her close against him. "Why can't you sleep, honey?" he asked gently, his breath stirring the tendril of hair that brushed her temple. "Can you tell me what's bothering you?"

"I'm just so tired," she whispered evasively, holding herself stiffly in the circle of his arms. "Too tired to sleep, I guess."

His left hand curved around her neck, the pressure of his thumb on her jaw urging her to rest her head in the hollow of his shoulder.

"You're so tense. Try to relax."

"But I can't," she muttered, clutching his lapel with her own left hand. "Let me take the pills, please, Ryan. I think I'll go crazy if I have to live through another sleepless night."

"But, Devon, you . . ."

"Please."

"Oh, all right, you can have one of them," he relented reluctantly, extracting the bottle from his left pocket. "Sit up a little bit. Can you reach the water?"

133

Nodding, she took the glass from the table, then leaned back from him slightly, wide beseeching eyes searching his lean face.

"The pills are so mild, Ryan. Please let me have two."

"One's all you're getting."

"But . . ."

"One, Devon, and that's final. I shouldn't even be giving you that."

"One won't put me to sleep," she said petulantly after swallowing the small blue pill. "I'll lay awake all night and it'll be all your fault."

"Just relax," he coaxed softly with an indulgent smile. "Rest your head on my shoulder. I won't leave you until I'm sure you can sleep."

"Really?" she asked hopefully, suddenly needing simply to be held by him. "You promise?"

"I promise," he whispered, brushing his lips against her hair, placing her hand near his collarbone and covering it with his own. "Now, relax."

"You'll stay even if I can't go to sleep all night?"

"I'll stay all night. Yes, I promise."

With a relieved sigh, she nuzzled her cheek against his shoulder, oddly finding security in the hard, warm strength of his body. A lazy little smile actually curved her lips as his hand clasped her waist, warming her skin through the thin cotton gown.

"I'm worried about you, Devon," he said very softly. "You're so thin, even thinner than you were before I brought you here, I think. Are you feeling all right? I mean, you don't think maybe you should see a doctor, do you?"

She tilted her head back to see him better, gazing with vague fascination at the strong line of his jaw and the barely discernible black stubble on mahogany skin.

"I don't think a doctor could do much for me," she murmured at last. Then a tiny frown of uncertainty

134

marred her brow. "Do . . . do you really worry about me, Ryan?"

Smiling down at her, he brushed rough fingertips along her cheekbone and then tugged gently at a flaxen tendril of hair. "Of course, I worry about you. I think that's fairly obvious."

"Not to me."

"Devon," he whispered admonishingly. "If it's any consolation to you, I'm not getting a lot of sleep lately either." Before she could answer, his mouth lowered to cover hers gently without the usual consuming passion.

Feeling curiously happy, Devon kissed him back, whispering his name. When her response hardened his lips, made them become more gently seeking, her hand slid inside his robe to move caressingly over his comforting warmth. He gathered her nearer; without hesitation, she relaxed, soft curves yielding to the masculine tautness of his body. Soon she wanted nothing more than to stay close to him forever.

After a few moments, however, Ryan released her mouth slowly, shaking his head. "Sleep, Devon. It's sleep you need right now," he said huskily, stilling her wandering hand. "You can hardly keep your eyes open."

He was right. A strange sense of contentment was spreading over her. With a sleepy sigh, she snuggled closer to him, nestling her face against his spice-scented brown throat. She allowed her eyes to flicker closed. Ryan's arms tightened around her, heightening her odd feeling of security. She murmured impulsively, "You . . . you wouldn't really try to take Jonathan away from me, would you?"

He tensed for a moment, then relaxed again, releasing his breath in a sigh. "Devon, you crazy child, is that what's bothering you tonight? If it is, you can stop worrying," he whispered, gently kissing her porcelain-smooth forehead. "Tell you what, let's make a new beginning and start trusting each other a little more. If you'll forgive me for accusing you of not wanting to have Jonathan, I'll forgive you for believing I might actually try to take him away from you. I couldn't do that. You're his mother and he loves you. I wouldn't have really tried to take him when we were still in Boston, and I won't try now."

"Ever?"

"Never, I promise."

Something instinctive made her believe him, and she lifted her hand to stroke his cheek. When he turned his head to brush his lips against her fingertips, she smiled drowsily. Then her hand floated down to curl lightly, trustingly, against his neck as she drifted into a deep sleep.

She awoke once in the darkness, realized she was in her bed, and almost imagined Ryan's arm resting heavily around her waist as his body curved protectively around her own. But when she awoke again to the clear light of day, she found to her dismay that she was alone.

Disappointed, she decided that she must have dreamed that he had stayed with her all night. After glancing at the clock and seeing that it was nearly ten, she scampered out of bed. She slowed down as she dressed, realizing that Jonathan had already been cared for. He must have been, or she certainly wouldn't have been allowed to sleep in so late—his demanding cry for food would have undoubtedly awakened her.

Ten minutes later, she took a fortifying breath and opened the door to the study, fully expecting to find Iris there with Jonathan and Ryan. To her great relief, father and son were alone.

As she approached the playpen, Ryan smiled up from his desk. "Are you feeling better this morning? Did you sleep well?"

"Yes," she murmured, her cheeks warming as she bent over the side of the playpen to touch Jonathan's chin with the tip of one finger. As he gurgled a welcome, she smiled at him, then glanced up rather shyly at Ryan. "Last night . . . I want to thank you for being so nice to me."

Something like a fleeting expression of anguish flickered on his face, then was gone, replaced by a rueful smile.

"I must not be nice to you often enough, if you have to thank me for last night."

"Oh, but I didn't mean . . ."

A dismissive wave of his hand silenced her. "It's all right. I thought we all might do something nice today, anyway. Maybe you would feel better if I didn't keep you cooped up in this study most of every day. How would you like to go on a picnic?"

"W . . . would Iris be going with us?" Devon asked hesitantly, dreading his answer. "I mean . . ."

"Iris left for home early this morning," Ryan answered, a hint of a smile tugging at the corners of his mouth as he rearranged some papers on his desk. "I thought we'd make it a family outing, so to speak. Just you and Jonathan and me. How about it?"

"Sounds like fun," she answered, barely able to suppress a sigh of relief. She smiled at him without meeting his eyes, afraid he would see how glad she was that Iris was gone and that he was actually being nice to her. It all seemed too good to be true, and although she had to wonder why he had suggested the picnic, she didn't want to question his motive now. She only wanted to accept what he offered without worrying. "Jonathan will like a picnic, I know. What time did you want to go?"

"I thought you could feed Jonathan early, say eleven thirty or so, then we could go. That way, you'll be able to relax and enjoy yourself."

Two hours later, as Devon and Ryan spread a blanket beneath the tall cottonwoods that edged the riverbank, she was relaxed. Jonathan, his tummy full, was cooing contentedly as she placed him in his stroller. She adjusted the backrest so that he was sitting up enough to see. Waving his arms excitedly, he gave her a bubbly smile, revealing a surprise—a tiny pearl-white tip on pink gum.

"A tooth! Oh, Ryan, look, he's getting his first tooth!"

Ryan bent down beside her, touching one tan finger against his son's fairer chin.

"Congratulations, young man," he murmured, smiling up at Devon after lightly ruffling Jonathan's dark, soft hair. "Since he's a bit young for champagne, I suppose we'll have to celebrate this milestone for him."

Surprise widened Devon's eyes. "You brought champagne? Pretty fancy for a picnic, isn't it?"

"But we're celebrating our new beginning." Ryan's smile deepened. "That makes this a special occasion."

And it was special. Finishing their meal with fresh fruit and cheese, plus another glass each of the sparkling champagne, Ryan and Devon sat silently on the blanket, gazing at the shallow river that wound its way past them. Beyond the copse, a brilliant red sun baked the sparsely grassy plain. But beneath the trees it was cool and soothingly shaded. Bees hummed as they flitted from occasional clusters of vibrant Texas bluebonnets to the scattered delicate pink prairie roses. Leaning back on her elbows, Devon looked up between the branches of the trees at a golden eagle that soared in graceful loops against the background of intensely blue sky.

"Don't see many of those anymore, especially around here," Ryan mused, watching the eagle's aerial acrobatics with her. "He's got to be a long way from home since there are no really high outcroppings of rock close by here. They usually choose high crags in canyon walls to build their aeries."

"He's magnificent, isn't he?" Devon whispered. "He makes flying look so easy." She gave Ryan an understanding smile. "Now I understand even better why environmental protection is so important to you. Everything about this land is too precious to be lost. It should stay the way it is, the way it's been for so long. I mean, do you realize that very little has changed since your great-grandmother first came here?"

Though Ryan nodded, he regarded her speculatively.

138

"Of course, you know she didn't exactly fall in love with this land at first sight. She even considered leaving Jacob Wilder and moving back to her family in Vermont."

"I know, but she didn't leave. According to her diary, she became very fond of life here and was extremely happy."

"Sometimes you seem happy here, too, Devon," Ryan announced softly, watching closely for her reaction to his remark. When she gave him a surprised glance, he smiled. "I don't think you're like my mother was, Devon. She was never happy one moment here. You're more like great-grandmother Louisa. You can adapt and even find beauty in a place you expected to be desolate and harsh." Still watching her, he slowly reached out a lean brown hand to cover her smaller one. He began to play idly with her fingertips. "I'm glad you can adapt, Devon."

Suddenly, everything seemed to be different. In a hushed silence—even the bees seemed to have ceased buzzing—Devon's heart began to beat swiftly in the near certainty that something unexpected and wonderful was about to happen. Excitement coursed through her veins. She found herself becoming lost in the darkness of Ryan's gaze. After brushing the tip of her tongue over suddenly dry lips, she breathed, "Why are you glad, Ryan?"

"Because—"

A sudden bubbly chuckle interrupted Ryan. Both he and Devon turned with some reluctance to look at their son. Then they had to exchange indulgent smiles. Jonathan had been approached by Maggie's yellow-and-cream Labrador retriever. The dog was gently nuzzling her soft black nose against the baby's round tummy. Jonathan giggled again; then, with a squeal of delight, he grasped the dog's silky ears.

"Oh, don't hurt her," Devon exclaimed softly, jumping up to disentangle the dog from her son's playful grip. Jonathan's chubby fingers loosened reluctantly. He wasn't eager to surrender such an appealing new plaything. But he cooed happily when Devon guided his small hand in gentle strokes over the dog's head and they were rewarded with a rapid wagging of tail. "You mustn't hurt the dog, honey. Be nice so she won't get frightened and snap at you."

"Oh, I doubt Georgia would ever bite him," Ryan reassured her, watching the scene from the blanket. "She's accustomed to Luke's kids pulling and tugging at her. She's learned to be pretty patient."

At the sound of his voice, Georgia rushed over to him, a dreamy ecstasy softening her brown eyes as he scratched behind her ears. Jonathan, however, howled indignantly because his new playmate had deserted him. He quieted as soon as Devon picked him up and began to rock him gently. Within a couple minutes, he was fast asleep. She lowered the backrest of the stroller and put him back in it.

"He's just all pooped out," she explained as she rejoined Ryan. Sitting down beside him, she grinned. "Of course, you really shouldn't have lured his doggie away from him, you villain."

Ryan laughed and stopped scratching Georgia's ears. As the dog ambled away to sprawl panting on the cool earth at the base of a tree, Devon sighed contentedly. For only the second time since she had first seen Ryan in that Boston restaurant, she felt almost completely relaxed. She realized what he had said was true. There were moments when she was actually happy here. Of course, Iris's absence from the ranch helped a great deal, but Devon didn't allow herself to dwell on thoughts of the older woman. Right now, she didn't want anything unpleasant to intrude on her sense of contentment.

As she idly brushed her hair back from her face, she sensed Ryan watching her and turned to smile at him. Her smile froze. Her hand went suddenly still. She imagined she saw warm affection in the dark depths of his eyes. He hadn't looked at her with such tenderness in over a year,

140

and she sat staring at him, nearly hypnotized. Then he moved swiftly, clasping her upper arms to lower her gently down onto the blanket. When he lowered his head to lightly kiss her, her heart actually skipped several beats.

"Marry me, Devon," he commanded softly. Pleasantly rough fingertips grazed the tender skin of her neck. Then he kissed her again, still gently though with a discernible passionate hardening of his lips. "Say yes."

"I can't say yes," she gasped, her heart triphammering against her breastbone. "I . . ."

"You could be happy here," he persisted, nibbling the soft lobe of one ear. "At least, say you'll think about it."

"I . . . I'll think about it," she agreed breathlessly, unable to resist him in this mood. Since last night, he had seemed so much like the Ryan she had fallen in love with in Boston. At this moment, she wished she could say she'd marry him. But caution still ran strong in her, too strong to be overcome in only a few minutes. Though she clasped her hands around his neck and nodded up at him, she warned, "I will think about it, I promise. But I may need a lot of time."

"Take all you need." Smiling enigmatically down at her, he was silent for several long moments. "Okay, time's up," he whispered abruptly, amusement glinting in his eyes. "So what's your decision?"

It was an old joke, but Devon laughed at it. As he laughed with her and lay down on his side, she allowed him to draw her close against him. They remained there for a long time, exchanging kisses that hinted at passion but were subdued and tenderly enchanting. Devon felt almost as if she had been transported back to their first evenings together in Boston when she had begun to fall in love with him. She felt she was where she belonged—in his arms, beneath the trees, being caressed by the ceaseless wind that had become a soft summer breeze bringing rising hope with it. Yet it was a hope she felt instinctively she should try to suppress. Deep inside, unstilled, was that

ever-present nagging fear that Ryan might hurt her very
badly again if she ever gave him the chance.

CHAPTER EIGHT

What should she do? That one little question tormented Devon for days after Ryan's proposal. Common sense told her that her answer should be a quick and simple no, but somehow she couldn't force herself to give that answer. Perhaps it was because he hadn't said "Marry me because we should get married" or "Marry me for Jonathan's sake." He had merely said "Marry me, Devon," and something in his tone had made it seem as if he really *wanted* her to say she would.

"Wishful thinking," Devon told herself repeatedly. He only felt he should marry her. It was Iris he really *wanted* to marry. Still, Devon couldn't say no. But she couldn't say yes, either. In a quandary, she almost wished he could and would force her to marry him. Yet Ryan did nothing to try to influence her decision. Apparently giving her the time she had said she needed to decide, he never mentioned the proposal. He only watched her expectantly whenever they were together in the days following the picnic. That silent, watchful waiting only added to her confusion.

Ryan's betrayal last year and his close relationship with Iris now made Devon fear she could never truly trust him, although she wanted to. And perhaps he could never really trust her either. Devon didn't know if he could or not. These days, she didn't seem to know anything at all for certain. Her mind was so jumbled with conflicting thoughts that she was even unable to concentrate on her writing.

By Wednesday afternoon, indecision was driving her practically batty. Hoping to escape her thoughts for at least an hour or so, she decided to go riding. In her room, she dressed in jeans and a light-blue Western shirt, then slid her feet into a pair of supple, tan leather boots. As the finishing touch, she put on the Western hat Ryan had insisted she buy in Corpus Christi. She knew she would need it. Here, the sun always blazed down fiercely.

Tucking a strand of hair back behind one ear, she surveyed her reflection in the mirror with a critical eye. Somehow, despite her proper attire, she just didn't look like she belonged in Texas. Perhaps it was her skin, she considered, probing her cheeks with light fingertips. Even with the light tan she had acquired, she still felt pale in comparison to everyone else on the ranch. Men, women, and children all were bronzed to a golden hue.

With a resigned sigh, she tipped her hat far back on her head. Leaving her room, she went through the house, looking for Maggie. She found her at last in the tiny sewing room adjacent to the kitchen. Leaning around the doorjamb, Devon fought to keep the smile on her lips when she saw Iris lounging lazily in a chair by the sewing machine. "Maggie, I thought I'd go for a short ride if you'd be willing to listen for Jonathan for me," Devon said. "Would you mind?"

"Of course not, dear," Maggie said readily. "But, are you riding alone?"

When Devon nodded, Iris suddenly hopped to her feet. "I'll go with you!" she declared eagerly. "I've been trying to think of something to do all day. We've never been riding together. It'll be such fun."

Oh, sure, a barrel of laughs, Devon thought morosely. Knowing she could hardly tell Iris to buzz off, she forced a wan smile and inclined her head in reluctant agreement.

A minute or so later, Devon was nearly ready to forsake

the idea of a ride altogether. As she and Iris walked from the house to the stable, the older girl launched into a monologue about some friends of hers in Dallas with whom she and Ryan had once spent a delightful weekend.

"It's a really nice day, isn't it?" Devon finally interrupted abruptly, hoping Iris would get the message and be quiet about her "fab" weekend with Ryan.

Amazingly, Iris did cease her soliloquy. She actually remained silent until they approached the paddock adjoining the stables where five or six horses nibbled the grass lazily. "You can ride Sorceress today. I imagine you usually do," Iris said with a shrug. "So do I, but we can't both ride her, can we?"

"No problem," Devon told her with a dismissive wave of her hand. "I always ride Ginger, anyway."

"Ginger? Really?" Iris tried without much success to hide her amusement. "But don't you think she's awfully slow?"

"She's fast enough for me," Devon said with a little laugh. "I didn't plan to race her."

Perhaps the involuntary hint of sarcasm in Devon's voice subdued Iris temporarily because she said very little as they saddled Ginger and Sorceress, then mounted and rode out north of the house. The girls took turns opening the paddock gates and when they left the last one behind to head toward the landing strip, Iris pulled up on the reins, frustrating the spirited black mare she rode. Obviously yearning for a hard run, Sorceress tossed her head and whinnied impatiently, but Iris was the consummate equestrienne and easily held her mount in check.

"Where do you usually ride?" she asked, stroking her mare's black, silky mane. "Anywhere special?"

Devon inclined her head westward. "I've always ridden toward the river."

"Always? Then let's go in a different direction today. Okay?"

"Lead on," Devon answered, touching her heels to Ginger's flanks.

For a while, Iris held Sorceress to a walk, but as they started along a path through prickly grasses, she suddenly gave the horse free rein. As the black mare leaped forward eagerly, Iris grinned back over her shoulder and tossed up her hand in a jaunty wave.

Devon wasn't left behind, however. Not to be outdone, Ginger broke into a gallop, fairly skimming over the matted grass of the path to keep pace with Sorceress.

It had been years since Devon had ridden a horse all out, but now she remembered what an exhilarating experience it was. The warm wind caressed her face, lifting her blond hair off her shoulders. She felt as if she were flying and appreciated Ginger's strong, even stride even if Sorceress was now out of sight beyond a low, rolling hill. Closing her eyes briefly, Devon inhaled the dry-grass fragrance of the air. She patted Ginger's neck as they slowed to a canter, then stopped by an outcropping of rock where Iris waited on Sorceress.

"Where have you been?" the older girl teased. "It took you so long to get here, I was beginning to think you might have turned back toward the house."

"Oh, Ginger's not that slow," Devon said, feeling compelled to defend her mount. "She's just a sweet, dependable horse." After glancing all around and seeing no familiar landmarks, she cast a questioning look in Iris's direction. "I sure hope you know where we are because I certainly have no idea. And Ryan told me never to ride beyond sight of the ranch."

"And do you always obey Ryan?" Iris asked, her tone no longer so cloyingly sweet.

"Shouldn't I?" Devon responded evenly. "He is the big man at Wilder Ranch, isn't he? Doesn't everyone call him boss?"

"Lots of ranchers are called boss."

146

"Oh? I didn't know that. But then, I am a newcomer here."

"And I know you must feel like a fish out of water," Iris declared undiplomatically. Her attempt at an understanding smile failed; there was a certain smugness to her expression instead. "I mean, this just isn't your kind of place. You must really hate it here."

"Oh, no, I don't hate it. I'm getting used to it actually. It's not nearly as desolate here as I thought it would be."

"Well, even so, you must be missing city living," Iris persisted, a frown appearing on her brow. "To tell you the honest truth, I'm surprised you aren't after Ryan to let you move to Corpus Christi at least. You could get yourself a nice apartment there and write."

"I can write just as well here on the ranch," Devon reminded her. "Better, probably, since my novel is set here."

"Are you saying you don't want to get away from here now?" Iris exclaimed, slapping the ends of her reins against the palm of one hand, exhibiting obvious agitation. "But you didn't even want to come in the first place! Why are you so willing to stay all of a sudden?"

"Well, I might as well be willing, hadn't I?" Devon responded dryly. "There's no use fighting the inevitable."

"And what exactly do you mean by that?" Iris snapped. "Just what's inevitable?"

Startled by the sudden interrogation, Devon jerked her head up to look at Iris. Her usual self-complacent expression had vanished. Irritation mingled with another indefinable emotion, sharpening Iris's features. She apparently realized how disgruntled she looked. A forced bland smile reappeared immediately, but for some reason, Devon felt uneasy. For a fraction of a second. she thought she detected a calculating glint of shrewdness in the other woman's eyes. "I only meant it's inevitable for Ryan to want Jonathan here with him. And where Jonathan stays, I have to stay," she explained at last. She turned one hand

147

palm upward, a resigned gesture. "Look, I know you can't be happy with this situation. You must be eager to get rid of me—something would probably be wrong with you if you weren't."

"Don't be absurd! I don't want to get rid of you," Iris protested too vehemently. "Whether you go or stay doesn't matter one little bit to me."

Devon shook her head. "Iris, you don't have to pretend that—"

"I'm not pretending! Your being here certainly doesn't bother me." Crimson color had mounted in Iris's cheeks, deepening the dark tint of her skin. With a toss of her head and a swirl of chestnut hair, she dug her heels into the black mare's flanks.

Watching her gallop away, Devon sighed, then followed at a more leisurely pace. Though the outburst from Iris had come somewhat unexpectedly, it was hardly surprising. Her patience must be wearing very thin, especially if Ryan had told her that Devon was presently considering his proposal of marriage. "How is all this going to end?" Devon muttered bleakly to herself. Then she resolutely thrust such thoughts to the back of her mind. After all, she had come riding so she could escape thinking about the tangle of relationships she was involved in.

The outcropping of rock extended farther than she had expected. When Ginger finally trotted sedately around the end, it was just in time for Devon to watch Iris disappear over a rise in the distance.

"Still miffed, I guess," she murmured, stroking Ginger's mane. "Well, we'd better try to catch up with her, hadn't we, girl?"

At the gentle tap of Devon's heels, the mare broke into a slow, easy canter. Yet when they reached the top of the gentle rise, they were confronted by a grove of deep-rooted, stunted mesquite trees, dwarfed by the dryness of the soil. Iris was nowhere in sight, but it seemed fairly obvious that she had taken the only really wide trail through the trees. Urging Ginger onward, Devon followed that trail also, relieved to be in partial shade for a while.

A few minutes later, however, she began to worry. Once the trail had meandered down through the copse of trees to the base of another low hill, it forked in two directions. Luckily, Sorceress had left tracks on the sparsely grassy dirt path to the right. Devon rode on, leaning forward in the saddle as Ginger climbed the rather steep side of the hill. At last they reached the crest.

Relief washed over Devon, then warred with impatience as she spotted Sorceress, a dark form on the distant horizon, lowering her head to graze as Iris stood still beside her, apparently waiting.

"Where the devil is she going? Nebraska?" Devon muttered aloud, urging Ginger on to a gallop. The wind felt delightful against her warm cheeks, but she was thirsty and tired and hoped Iris would be ready to start toward home very soon. As the glare of the sun burned into her eyes, Devon tilted her hat forward on her forehead and guided Ginger carefully over the rough terrain. It wasn't until she had almost reached her destination that she looked straight out into the glaring sun again. When she did, she swore impatiently.

What she had thought was Sorceress was in reality a stray steer. It looked up at her with baleful brown eyes, apparently not exactly thrilled with solitude, then began to munch again on the roots of the tall clump of grass Devon had assumed was Iris.

"Hell and damnation," Devon muttered, turning Ginger around, intending to go back the way they had come. Another surprise awaited her, however. There were several rolling hills in the distance and she had no idea which one she had ridden over. All she could do was to head back toward the one in the center and hope she would find Iris loitering somewhere nearby.

An hour later, after riding from hill to hill and never seeing one glimpse of the older girl, Devon decided to find her own way back home. Seeing traces of tracks on one vaguely familiar path, she entered a stand of mesquite, nearly losing her hat to low-hanging branches several times before she made it through. Out in the open again, however, she realized she must have taken a wrong turn in the maze because she had never seen this place before. Instead of finding the outcropping of rock she had expected, she faced another low rise. At the top of that, she stared dismally at rolling prairie that stretched out before her. Unfortunately, she could see neither river nor ranch nor anything else even vaguely familiar.

"Let's try again, girl," she said softly, turning back.

A half hour later, Devon finally admitted she was lost. She had ridden in every direction, but nothing looked familiar and now she was hopelessly turned around. Hot and dusty, her throat aching for a cool swallow of water, she patted Ginger's neck, sighing when she noticed the horse was sweating profusely.

"Poor old girl," she murmured comfortingly. "You're used to nice easy outings, aren't you, not frantic gallops through the wilderness? Well, I'm sorry. I just didn't expect to lose sight of Iris like that."

Maybe Iris had planned it that way, she thought musingly, then pushed that suspicion aside. Surely they had become separated purely by accident.

"Well, since we're lost anyway, we might as well look for water," she said aloud. "No use going thirsty while we wait for someone to find us."

Actually, Ginger found the water. After trotting along a dry creekbed for a couple of miles, she jerked up her head with a snort, and increasing her pace without encouragement, headed straight for a small waterhole. Sparkling water from deep underground had made an inviting pool. As Ginger began making the most of it, Devon swung down from the saddle. Kneeling beside the water, she scooped up a handful and touched the tip of her tongue to it cautiously. Wrinkling her nose, she allowed the water to trickle slowly between her fingers. As she had suspected, it was stagnant and almost too full of minerals for human consumption. Only animals would want to drink much of it.

Suddenly, with lightning speed, a horned dragon, an ugly orange-and-black lizard, scuttled past Ginger's bent head. The mare reared, then was off and running in a flash, not even hesitating when Devon called her back.

"You traitor," Devon shouted after her. "And to think I told Iris you were dependable!"

As Ginger became a mere speck in the distance, the lonely silence of the plain suddenly enveloped Devon, and she shivered, despite the heat. Wondering if the horse would find her way home, she knelt by the pool again to splash water against her cheeks. She stood up, rubbing her wet hands over her neck and looking around for a good place to wait until she was found. There were no good places out here, she finally decided. With a resigned shrug, she headed for the only shade she saw, a scruffy-looking cottonwood tree.

The tree was much farther away than she had imagined. By the time she was halfway to it, her clothes were drenched with perspiration. Unfortunately, she had left her hat dangling from the pommel of Ginger's saddle, and now, without it, the sun's rays beat down on her head until it began to feel as if it might explode. The tree before her became a blurry shape as a sudden dizziness weakened her, making her nauseated.

At last she reached her destination and sank down, resting against the rough, furrowed trunk. Spots were dancing before her eyes, heightening her nausea, but when she tried to draw her knees up so she could rest her head on them, her legs cramped, compelling her to stretch them out on the ground again.

She felt horrid. Despite the heat, her skin was cold and clammy. Her head throbbed, and she would have given anything for a swallow of water to bathe the dusty, dry ache in her throat.

By the time the sun was setting, Devon's thoughts weren't completely rational. Though she was too weak to move, she wanted to, imagining she would soon be seeing snakes slithering freely over her outstretched legs. She shivered at the fanciful thought, closing her eyes. When she opened them again later, darkness had fallen. A coyote howled plaintively in the distance and was answered by several others. Did packs of coyotes ever attack people? she wondered with a shudder.

Leaning her head back, she stared up at the clear blue velvet sky, focusing her gaze on Vega, summer's brightest star. It twinkled down at her in almost mocking silence. All around the restless wind whispered eerily, the way it had whispered and haunted Ryan's great-grandmother's early years on the Texas plain. What relentless loneliness and isolation Louisa Wilder must have felt. For the first time, Devon experienced the devastating sense of isolation the wind carried with it; she could almost imagine she was the only person left in the entire world. Tears pricked behind her eyelids. Maybe Ryan wouldn't even come out here and try to find her. Allowing her to remain lost would certainly simplify his life. He would have Jonathan all to himself then, and he could marry Iris anytime he pleased.

Although Devon realized she was succumbing to a bad case of self-pity, she couldn't seem to staunch the sudden flow of tears. Sniffling weakly, she turned her head toward an abrupt, strange roar. It seemed to be getting increasingly louder. What animal sounded like that? she wondered vaguely, watching with only mild interest two fiery, glowing spots looming larger and larger in the darkness. It took another minute for her disoriented brain to realize it was a Jeep she was seeing and hearing. Even after she had recognized that fact, it took all her energy to drag herself up and stagger away from the tree to where she might be spotted by the unknown driver. The headlights turned toward her a few seconds later. She closed her eyes against their harsh glare, swaying in the wind where she stood.

"My God, Devon!" Ryan exclaimed immediately after the roar of the Jeep's engine ceased. Running to her, he gripped her upper arms tightly. "Are you all right?" When she shook her head in answer to his question, he drew her roughly into his arms, smoothing her hair back from her clammy cheeks. "You crazy little nitwit, don't you have any sense?" he chided urgently. "Why did you wander off that way? Don't you know people can die out here?"

"Why didn't Iris wait for me?" she retorted raspingly. "She knew I didn't know where I was."

Walking her toward the Jeep, he said softly, "She thought you were right behind her."

"Iris doesn't think," Devon muttered indiscreetly. "She's an imbecile."

"But she's not the one who got lost, is she?" Ryan muttered back.

Before Devon could think of a snappy answer, darkness began edging in on her eyes and her legs went rubbery. She was falling, and the last thing she felt before slipping into unconsciousness were Ryan's arms closing securely around her.

CHAPTER NINE

According to the doctor, Devon was suffering with a severe case of heat exhaustion. Lying in her bed, she heard his diagnosis above the thunderous roaring in her head. After she felt the sharp pinprick of the injection he administered, however, she knew very little else for the next thirty-six hours. There would never be more than vague recollections of being fed some warm liquid at intervals and occasionally being led to the bathroom.

Re-entering the world was painful. When she awakened, it was to the grayer light of morning. Her head still ached, though fortunately not nearly as severely as it had. To make matters worse, she barely had a chance to open her eyes before a deep, insidious weariness settled within her. All the fight seemed to have deserted her along with physical stamina. She felt weak and helpless.

When Devon struggled up to prop herself on one elbow, only Emily, Maggie's shy housemaid, was in the room. Instead of speaking, she ran out the door, calling for her mistress. Her head throbbing painfully, Devon lowered herself back down on the pillow, wondering if Ryan was still disgusted with her for getting lost. Probably. But he might at least be fair enough to lay some of the blame on Iris for stupidly assuming that Ginger could keep pace with Sorceress. He might not be that fair, though; Devon feared he wouldn't and sighed dejectedly as she stared up at the ceiling. At the sound of a light tap on her open door, she lifted her head off the pillow.

"So you *are* finally awake," Maggie said cheerfully, coming across the room to stand smiling by the bed. "My, you had us all plenty worried Wednesday night. We were beginning to think we weren't going to find you."

"I'm sorry," Devon murmured. "I suppose all the hands had to be sent out to search for me, didn't they?"

"Well, we certainly couldn't leave you out there, could we?"

"How's Jonathan?" Devon asked urgently, a sudden overwhelming need to hold her son sweeping over her. "Can I see him? Has he been upset because I've not been looking after him? Where is he now?"

"He's fine. And he's with Ryan right now. Yes, he did miss you, but Ryan brought him in to see you several times and that seemed to satisfy him for at least a little while."

"Oh, I have to see him." Devon's eyes glimmered. "Please, would you bring him in here to me?"

"Of course, but after you've had something to eat."

"But . . ."

"It won't be much. Just some more of the broth we gave you yesterday."

"Yesterday?" Devon exclaimed. "What day is this? Not Friday, surely! You can't mean I slept through two whole nights and a day!"

"Yes, you did, but the doctor said you needed the rest. And I must say you did look very ill when Ryan brought you in Wednesday night. There didn't seem to be a drop of blood left in you—you were that pale. But then, heat exhaustion *is* very serious business."

"What about Ginger? Did she make it back home okay?" Devon asked, genuinely concerned. "I was afraid she might be as lost as I was."

"She straggled in just before dark," Maggie said, then a frown puckered her brow. "Did that mare throw you, Devon? I want you to tell me if she did."

"Oh, but she didn't. Really. We ran across a waterhole and while she was drinking, a lizard zipped right past her

155

head. It spooked her, and she bolted before I could catch the reins. Ginger wouldn't throw anybody, I'm sure. She's very gentle—she's just not as dependable as I thought."

Maggie hardly seemed to notice Devon's wry smile. She hovered hesitantly for a moment on the brink of speaking before finally voicing her question. "Could you tell me why you didn't stay with Iris? I mean, I know you're aware of how dangerous it is to wander off alone out there. I was wondering if you were upset with Iris for some reason. I hope not. I know how much she wants to be your friend."

Sighing, Devon massaged her temples wearily. Simply the thought of Iris was enough to make the pain in her head considerably worse. Obviously Maggie recognized that. "We can talk about it later, dear. Your head is bothering you, isn't it? The doctor did say it might hurt for several days."

"He knew what he was talking about, then," Devon said with a rueful smile. "It does still hurt, though not so much as before."

Nodding, Maggie waved her hand toward a bottle of pills on the bedside table. "He left some pain medication for you. You're to take it only after meals, though." At the sudden clattering noise in the hall, Maggie turned in her chair and smiled as Emily came into the room, carrying a rattan lap tray. "Ah, here's your broth now. Can you feed yourself or would you like for me to help you?"

"I'll feed myself," Devon said hastily, sitting up with careful deliberation to avoid jarring her head. Pushing a pillow behind her back, she rested against the headboard, closing her eyes against the slight dizziness that accompanied her movement.

"Are you sure you don't need my help, dear?" Maggie asked as she sat the tray on the bed over Devon's lap. "I certainly don't want you overdoing."

Devon shook her head determinedly. "Thanks, but I want to feed myself." After sipping a spoonful of the delicious chicken-barley broth, she glanced at Maggie. "When can I get out of this bed? I've been in here too long already. Could I get up after I've eaten?"

"Lord, no! Three full days bed rest the doctor said, so don't you start being a difficult patient." Maggie eyed her sternly, then gave a little sigh. "I was afraid this climate wouldn't be good for your health. You're just too delicate for a harsh place like this, and I worry about you."

"Don't. I'm not all that delicate, I assure you," Devon said emphatically. "Heat exhaustion could happen to anybody who got too much sun."

"Yes, I guess so," Maggie agreed, though she didn't seem entirely convinced. Then she smiled again. "Well, right now you should only think about regaining your strength. So, come on, eat all the broth."

After Devon finished eating, Maggie removed the tray, then dispensed one yellow headache capsule.

"Now, that should help ease the pain," she said, bending over to straighten the bedclothes. "It will probably make you very drowsy, though, but sleep is what you need."

"No, I *need* to see Jonathan," Devon declared. "And I don't want to go to sleep again before I do. Please, could you bring him in now? But before you do, could you hand me my brush? I feel like my hair's a real rat's nest."

"It's not so bad, dear, just a bit mussed," Maggie assured her. But she fetched the brush anyway, then walked toward the door. "I'll be back with Jonathan in a second."

Simply lifting her arm to run the brush through her hair tired Devon. When she had smoothed the silken strands around her shoulders she let her hand drop limply to her lap and closed her eyes. The moment she heard activity in the hall, however, she sat up straight, unwilling to show Maggie how weak she really was.

But it wasn't Maggie who appeared in the doorway a few seconds later. Carrying Jonathan, Ryan stepped into the room, his gaze sweeping over Devon with a dark intensity that made her pulses race. As he approached the bed, she broke the disturbing eye contact and focused all her attention on her son.

"Come here, sweetheart," she murmured, holding out her arms. At the first sight of her, a swift, joyous smile appeared on Jonathan's chubby face. Devon cradled him close, brushing her lips across his smooth forehead. When he clutched a fistful of her thin blue lawn nightgown, she turned her eyes to Ryan again as he sat down in the chair by the bed.

"Maggie tells me your head is still aching," he said quietly, stroking his tan cheek with one lean finger. "Do you think I should have the doctor fly back out here and check you?"

"Oh, no, I'll be fine, I'm sure. In fact, I feel like getting out of bed right now."

The lie was obviously unconvincing. Leaning forward, resting his elbows on his knees, Ryan smiled indulgently. "I don't think you're ready to get up yet. You better rest and let us take care of you for a few days longer, at least."

"But Jonathan . . ."

"Jonathan is just fine. I keep him in the study with me most of the time, and if he gets cranky, Maggie's happy to play with him."

"Well, you don't have to make it sound like I'm not even needed," she said grumpily, unreasonably irritated by his answer. She glared indignantly at him when he grinned. "What's so funny?"

"You are," he answered candidly. "You must be feeling better because you're very touchy. But I didn't mean you're not needed; I think you know you are."

How the devil was she supposed to know that? she wondered, her mood a combination of depression and defensive anger. Maggie's comments had upset her more than she had realized. Knowing Ryan's own stepmother thought she was completely ill-suited for the life here was discouraging enough. She hadn't needed to be chided for not being friendlier to Iris. Without warning, an abject feeling of total desolation settled in her chest. But she would have died before showing anybody how totally alone she felt, especially Ryan. Lifting her chin, she muttered, "I suppose you're still furious with me for getting lost and causing everyone so much trouble?"

His narrowed eyes flicked swiftly over her, then he shrugged. "Let's just say you better never do it again or I'll turn you over my knee."

"I'd love to see you try," she challenged beneath her breath as she felt heat rise to her cheeks. Deciding to ignore Ryan, she spent the next several minutes talking to Jonathan. He was so obviously glad to be with her again that she felt somewhat less alone. At least the child loved her, even if his father never would.

Too soon, however, Devon became tired and a little giddy as a result of the pain medication she had taken. Still, she protested when Ryan stood up and said she should rest.

"No, let Jonathan stay just a little longer, please. I'm not tired, really."

"Then why do your eyes keep closing every few seconds?" he countered, gathering his son up into his arms. "For once, Devon, give in to something. You're sleepy, so go to sleep. That's what you need."

"I guess you're right," she agreed reluctantly, stifling a yawn as she wriggled down beneath the sheet. Her blond hair fanned out around her face on the pillow and drowsy eyes looked up at Ryan and their son. She smiled hopefully. "You'll bring him back when I wake up again, though, won't you? Promise?"

"I promise," Ryan whispered, leaning down to touch his mouth gently to hers. "Rest now, Devon."

Feeling oddly content, she turned her cheek into the pillow and closed her eyes.

When Devon awakened several hours later, early-afternoon sun filtered through the small spaces between the slats of the blinds covering the window. With a lazy stretch, she looked around the darkened room. Her yawn ended prematurely and she went perfectly still as she saw Ryan sitting in the chair beside her bed, watching her awaken. Something akin to tender amusement warmed his eyes to deep blue pools. Her heart began to thud with near breathtaking rapidity. Heat rose in her cheeks; she felt an abrupt, indescribable vulnerability knowing he had been there, observing her while she slept. To mask her discomfort, she hastily averted her eyes while shifting her pillow up against the headboard. She sat up in bed, her headache mercifully eased, and gave Ryan a hesitant, questioning smile.

He interpreted her puzzled expression correctly and explained his presence. "When Jonathan began to fret after lunch, I brought him in here where he could see you. He finally went to sleep, so Maggie came and took him to his crib to finish his afternoon nap."

"But you stayed?"

Ryan smiled somewhat sheepishly, then leaned over to pick up something from the floor by his chair. It was the first fifty pages or so of Devon's manuscript. "You're making fast progress, aren't you?"

Devon's eyes widened in surprise. "You read it? I didn't think you'd be interested."

"I couldn't resist. It was laying on your dresser so I just picked it up. I didn't think you'd mind." As she shook her head, he was silent, almost tensely silent. He idly thumbed through the typed pages before looking directly into her eyes, his expression serious. "It's excellent, Devon. I understand better now why your writing is so important to you. You *do* have a talent that shouldn't be wasted."

"You really like it?" she said, scarcely able to believe he had praised her work and unreasonably happy that he had. For that reason, she had to be certain he had really meant what he said. "You're sure you really think it's good?"

An indulgent smile curved his lips as he nodded. "I'm sure. It's a terrific beginning, Devon. I hadn't realized you were writing something so realistic. I don't claim to be a literary critic, of course, but you seem to have captured the awesome loneliness pioneer women must have felt when they first came to the Texas prairie. The way you use the constant sound of the wind to sort of symbolize the sense of absolute isolation your heroine felt is very effective. I can feel everything with her. Now I understand better how lost a woman can feel when she first comes here. I'd read my great-grandmother's diary, of course, but you've expanded her thoughts and feelings and given your heroine such depth that . . . Well, suffice it to say that I'm looking forward to seeing how you end the story. I hope you'll let me read it when you've finished."

"Of c . . . course," she whispered haltingly, unable to hide the pleasure she felt. "Actually, I'd like very much for you to read it as I go along. Since it's set in Texas, you could help me a great deal. You know, by checking for authenticity."

"Anytime," he agreed, then he grinned. "To tell the truth, I'm still surprised you ever picked Texas as your setting, since you were none too eager to come."

"Oh, but you were right. This part of Texas does grow on you," she admitted softly. "Somehow there's beauty in the very starkness of it, and now . . . well, I think you know I'm beginning to like it here."

His dark eyebrows lifted inquiringly. "Even after getting lost the other day?"

"That's just it. I'm not so sure I got lost," she blurted out impulsively. "I mean, I've been wondering if maybe I was led astray."

Ryan frowned. "What do you mean by that exactly?"

His deep voice was edged with a certain intimidating hardness, and Devon's heart sank. But inherent honesty forced her to continue. "Well, I just suspect . . . I mean, it's occurred to me that maybe Iris could have deliberately let me lose my way."

"I find that very hard to believe, Devon," he answered grimly, a flicker of displeasure graying his eyes. "Why would Iris purposely let you get lost? That doesn't make any sense to me. Worried as she's been about you the last couple of days, I can assure you your suspicions are wrong. I've known Iris all my life, and I can't imagine her doing anything like that."

"But . . ."

"She'd like to be your friend, but you seem to do your best to avoid her," he chastised softly. "Don't you think it would be better all the way around if you tried a little harder to like her?"

Looking down, Devon stared blindly at her hands resting in her lap. "You're probably right, Ryan," she murmured. "And I guess I can try to be friendlier to her."

"Good." He leaned forward in his chair, smiling again. "You could begin now, if you want to. She's been wanting to come in here and see you. How about it?"

Unable to face that prospect yet, Devon pressed trembling fingers against her forehead. "Couldn't we postpone that? My head's beginning to hurt again."

"I see. Well, I'll leave so you can rest," he said, his tone cool again as he rose to his feet. "Try to go back to sleep if you can."

Devon nodded. As he left the room, closing the door behind him, loneliness engulfed her again. Nothing had changed. Ryan trusted Iris in a way he had never trusted her. Faced with that fact, Devon realized she would only be courting heartache if she married him. Besides, he hadn't exactly reissued his proposal this afternoon. Maybe by now he was even regretting ever asking her to marry him.

By resting in between, Devon was able to feed Jonathan all his meals on Sunday. It was good to be somewhat active again, to know Maggie could no longer see her as a completely helpless invalid. Even being up and about again didn't make Sunday a terrific day, however. Iris was still firmly entrenched in the guest room, and her presence at the ranch always put a damper on everything for Devon. She had thought time would make Iris more bearable, but it hadn't worked out that way. The old cliché about familiarity breeding contempt applied perfectly in this situation. Devon knew it would only get worse the longer she stayed. She wanted to leave, yet ached at the thought of leaving. How could she go through the rest of her life knowing what it might have been like to live here with Ryan, to have been his wife? If she had never seen this place, imagining a life with him would have been far more difficult, but now through all the coming years she would remember the ranch and know that Iris was sharing everything with him. Jonathan, of course, would return for visits, but she would probably never come back again.

It would be painful to walk away and know there would be no returning. And surely it would be something like dying to leave Ryan and know that there was no longer *any* hope that he might begin to love her. She had hoped he would. She had to admit to herself that deep down inside her she had harbored the foolish dream that somehow everything would work out right. Nothing had, though, and inexplicably the bout of heat exhaustion had made her think that none of it ever would work out the way she wanted.

Now the only real peace she found was in sleep, and for that reason she didn't rejoin Maggie, Ryan, and Iris in the living room after putting Jonathan to bed Sunday night. Instead, she wondered into her room to stand aimlessly for a few minutes before mustering the energy to take a bath.

As she soaked in a tub of soothingly warm, bath-salt-scented water, she told herself she wouldn't be missed by the others, anyway. Though Ryan was always discreet in her presence and never gave a clue as to his true feelings

163

for Iris, Devon sensed a warmth between them, an almost conspiratorial warmth that excluded her as if she didn't exist. So even though they were usually discreet, it hurt a great deal to see them together, knowing they both must be wishing they could be alone.

Well, they had a chance to be alone tonight, Devon thought as she stepped from her bath, wrapping herself in a thick blue bath towel. With her out of the way, Maggie had probably been perceptive enough to retire also to give them time alone together. Would Ryan spend the night in Iris's bed? Did he ever? Devon didn't know for certain nor did she want to know. The mere possibility that he did was torture enough.

After slipping into her sheerest white cotton gown, brushing her hair, and cleaning her teeth, Devon walked back into her bedroom. The night was unusually warm. Though she was extremely tired, she didn't really feel sleepy and she knew it would be useless to go to bed.

Hoping a few minutes of fresh air would make her drowsy, she stepped out of her room onto the private screened veranda. The flagstone floor was cold beneath her bare feet as she went to stand in the corner where vines heavy with fragrant white moonflowers climbed a support post.

A bird sang out sadly from the treetops. As Devon drew a long, shuddering breath in answer, the sharp snap and sizzle of a match being struck spun her around with a silent gasp.

Ryan stood framed in the doorway to his room, his bare torso gleaming like copper in the lamplight spilling around him. Devon stood perfectly still, not certain he had noticed her in the shadows.

"What's wrong, Devon?" he asked softly, ending her speculation as he started toward her. "Can't you sleep?"

"I . . . well, I haven't tried yet," she answered from her dark corner. "It was just so warm that . . . that I decided to come out here for some air."

His hands thrust deep into his trouser pockets, he stopped a foot or so from her. "I still have those sleeping tablets if you think you might need one."

"No. No, thanks," she murmured rather reluctantly. The assurance of sleep one of the tiny blue pills would have provided was tempting, but not so tempting that she would willingly show him any sign of weakness. Shaking her head resolutely, she half turned. "No, I won't need one."

He moved close behind her, his voice low and melodious, his warm breath caressing her bare shoulder. He murmured, "I expected you to come back to join us in the living room. Why didn't you?"

Devon tensed, trying to ignore the tantalizing warmth that emanated from his body. "I was tired."

"But now you can't sleep. Why?" One hand gently gripped a shoulder and turned her to him. The fingers of the other brushed across her brow. "Is it your head? Is it hurting?" When she shook her head, he lifted her chin with one finger. "Then tell me why you can't sleep. Tell me what you're feeling."

"N . . . nothing," she lied breathlessly. "I don't feel any way or anything."

"Don't you? Not even this?" he whispered, deliberately brushing his hands down over the enticing swell of her breasts. When she trembled, his fingers began to explore their perfect roundness. A slight triumphant smile curved his firm lips as aroused nipples surged hard against his palms. "Yes, you do feel something, don't you, and you feel it every minute of every day, just the way I do. How long did you think we could go on this way, sleeping in separate rooms, yet only a few feet from each other? You know, don't you, that I've wanted to come to you every night?"

She couldn't answer. Her heart seemed to beat frantically somewhere in her throat, and she could hardly breathe.

She could only look up at him, mesmerized by the light that shone in his half-closed eyes.

His hands spanned her waist and he drew her close against him, lowering his head to whisper into her ear. "Remember that night, Devon? Remember what we had together? Remember how nervous you were the first time? But by the time morning came . . . You remember, don't you?"

"Yes," she gasped against his shoulder, her legs going weak with the memory. When his hands closed on her hips to press her to him and she felt the throbbing evidence of his passion, an intoxicating heat coursed through her body. Almost of their own volition, her fingers feathered over the racing pulse in his throat, then up to his hair, tangling in the clean, vibrant thickness. She clung to him, trembling, unbearable needs rising feverishly in her until every nerve, every inch of her body burned.

"Yes, you do remember, don't you? And you've never felt that way with anyone else since, have you, Devon?"

Seduced by his voice and the hard, demanding strength of his body, she shook her head, shuddering as his mouth tasted the creamy skin of her throat. Waiting with aching anticipation for his kiss, she moved against him and found delight in his hard, upsurging response.

"Remember how you feel when we make love?" he whispered against her eagerly parting lips. "Do you remember?"

"Yes. Oh, *yes*," she gasped, wrapping her arms around his neck. "I remember. Oh, Ryan, stop talking and just kiss me. *Please.*"

With a low groan of satisfaction, his mouth covered hers, his tongue probing the sweet, softly textured flesh of her lips as his oddly unsteady hands explored the curves of her body.

"Devon," he muttered roughly. "God forgive me, I can't keep away from you." He swiftly unfastened the tiny buttons of her gown. Then he pushed her from him slightly, slipping the narrow straps down her shoulders and off her arms.

The sheer white cotton drifted down around her feet. A gentle breeze caressed Devon's bare skin. As Ryan's dark eyes swept hungrily over her, an erotic thrill pulsated inside her. Exposed to his passionate gaze, she felt delightfully vulnerable. She ached to be touched again.

"Exquisite," he whispered hoarsely, reaching out to cup her straining breasts in his hands. "Your skin is absolutely exquisite, like warm ivory satin. You feel so good, Devon," he murmured, "I could go on touching you forever."

Wordlessly, Devon moved into his arms, breathing in his fresh, masculine scent as she trailed seductive, teasing kisses across his chest. As his seeking hands slipped beneath the waistband of her panties, she tilted her head back, gazing up at him, signaling total submission with a soft, tremulous sigh.

Muttering her name, he swept her swiftly up into his arms to carry her into her room and place her down on the bed. He switched out the lamp, then quickly shed his trousers. Lowering his lean body down to cover hers, he cupped her face in both his hands, his mouth claiming hers in a possessively devouring kiss.

Devon arched her slight body against the irresistible hardness of his, allowing his muscular thigh to part her legs. Her hands kneaded the muscles of his back, pressing him down to her as the kisses they exchanged deepened to intimate explorations.

"You're a delight," he whispered, nibbling the soft lobe of one ear. "Oh, God, I need you, Dev. I want you so much."

Dev. He had called her Dev only once before. That night, in the first poignant moment of possession, he had whispered, "You're mine now, Dev, mine forever."

And she was his. She had known it then and she knew it now. Though a part of her brain urged caution, his voice, his hands, and his lithe strength were such compelling inducements to surrender that she was swept away into a sensual world beyond all reasonable thought.

She caressed his chest, her nails catching in the fine hair. She lifted her mouth to his again, whispering against his lips, "I need you, too, Ryan."

Wrapping the silken swathe of her hair around one hand, he tilted her head back, exposing the slender arch of her neck to his marauding mouth. The tip of his tongue probed the wildly beating pulse, then blazed a burning trail downward to seek the scented hollow at the base of her throat. Strong, even teeth nipped at her.

Devon was on fire for him. Sparkles of delight danced over her skin, shimmering opalescently in the pale moonlight. Gazing up through the feathery fringe of thick lashes, she drew a sharp breath, mesmerized by the passion in his eyes as he looked down at her. Her fingers spread open against the rippling muscles of his chest until his hands covered the taut mounds of her breasts, his palms brushing with deliberate, evocative slowness over the tender peaks. Then, breathing his name, her own hands covered his to press them down roughly against her yielding softness.

Ryan groaned. His firm, demanding mouth sought her parted lips again, twisting them slightly beneath his. Aflame with desire, Devon begged, "Make love to me, Ryan. Please, *now.*"

For a moment, his mouth took hers with bruising force, then he tensed and lifted his head. "Oh, Dev, I need to make love to you, but, God, I just can't . . . I might make you pregnant again."

"I don't care," she whispered urgently, trailing enticing little kisses over the contours of his shoulders. "Just love me, please. I don't care if you do make me pregnant."

"Dev, no! I can't take that chance. I promised . . ." With a muffled exclamation, he dragged himself away from her to sit on the edge of the bed, raking his fingers through his hair.

Devon went rigid, humiliation burning away all desire. He promised . . . Promised what? She knew. Oh, she knew. He had promised Iris he would never make love to her, Devon, again, that he would never chance complicating their lives further with another child. He had wanted her, but not so much that he had forgotten his promise to Iris. Suddenly, Devon wanted to flail at him with her fists. Instead, she fought back her hurt and anger until she felt she might explode.

"Devon, *Devon*," Ryan muttered gruffly, turning and reaching out to lay a hand on her thigh. "I . . ."

"No!" Shrinking away, she hurled his hand from her leg, her eyes glimmering in the semidarkness. "Don't you touch me!" she whispered almost hysterically. "Don't you ever, *ever* touch me again!" Turning over onto her side, she buried her face in the crumpled sheet. After a moment, she felt Ryan get up, then she heard him walk out of the room.

A desolate cry was muffled in the softness of Devon's pillow. She pressed her palms hard against throbbing temples, wondering how she had managed to let him make a fool of her again. All his honeyed words about new beginnings, all his gentleness during their picnic had meant nothing. *Nothing.* He had only asked her to marry him because of their son. Idiot that she was, though, she had longed to believe he wanted *her*. Well, tonight he had proven beyond a shadow of a doubt that she wasn't the woman he wanted. It was Iris who came first with him. Always Iris.

CHAPTER TEN

The next evening, Devon found her bottle of prescribed sedatives in the top drawer of a dresser in Ryan's room. She tapped one pill out onto her palm, replaced the bottle, and left quickly and quietly. In her own room again, she put the tablet on the bedside table with a sigh of relief. Thank God, she had been able to get it; there would have been no sleep for her tonight if she hadn't.

Lowering herself wearily onto the bed, she curled up on her side, pressing her palms against her temples. Her head had ached hideously all day until now it was beginning to make her feel nauseated. She was glad to be in her room where she no longer had to pretend she was okay.

The day had begun early and dragged along. When Devon had left her room at seven in the morning, Ryan was already on his way to Houston. Anxious as she had been to know why he had gone, she couldn't ask anyone. Maggie seemed to assume she knew, and nothing on earth would have induced Devon to question Iris.

Why had he gone, though? she wondered again as she massaged her temples. Was his sudden departure somehow related to what had happened between them last night? Perhaps he had felt too guilty to face Iris this morning. Or perhaps he had simply desired escape from the entire intolerable situation for a few days. Devon couldn't blame him if he had. She too desired escape, and for longer than a few days. After showing Ryan all too blatantly how she felt last night, she could hardly bear the thought of facing him again. There was only so much humiliation a person could stand; Devon felt she had already been pushed far beyond her limit.

She could take Jonathan and run. That idea had been in her mind all day, but she couldn't imagine how she could get away. Ryan had the plane. Even if he hadn't taken it, Luke would never have flown her anywhere without permission. Driving to the nearest town was out. Maggie would suspect something if she suggested taking a baby on such a trek in this heat. That left no way to go. Yet there had to be a way out of this mess, she thought desperately. Maybe when her headache was gone, her brain would function better, and she would be able to devise a plan. It was something to hope for anyway, and at the moment, she was ready to cling to any hope she could find, however slight.

If only she could relax . . . Turning over onto her back, Devon pressed shaky fingers against closed eyes to counteract the aching, burning pressure behind them. It didn't help. Just as she began to try massaging her neck instead, there was a knock on the door. Iris popped into the room, her cheery smile changing to an exaggerated expression of concern. "Oh, don't you feel well, honey?" she asked, tiptoeing to the bed. "I was afraid maybe you didn't. You've just been so quiet today. You didn't even do any writing, so something *must* be wrong. What is it?"

"My head," Devon said stiffly, closing her eyes in an obvious hint. "It might go away if I could rest quietly, so . . ."

"Oh, I only wanted to talk to you a minute," Iris said, recognizing the hint, but not letting it bother her in the least. Sitting down, she assumed an attractive pose on the edge of the chair, a small frown knitting her smooth, dark brow. "I was hoping you might know why Ryan went to Houston. I mean, he told me he was going; he came to my room in the middle of the night to say good-bye, of course.

171

But he wouldn't tell me precisely why he was going. And he did seem a little upset."

Good, Devon thought with grim satisfaction. He deserved being upset. No, he deserved being utterly miserable after what he had done to her last night. She could only hope he went through the rest of his life feeling like the world's sorriest cad. Unable to voice that hope to Iris, however, she shrugged instead. "I'm not sure why he went. Maybe to give a lecture or . . ."

"Oh, no, he didn't go to lecture. Actually, I wondered if maybe the two of you had decided to put an end to this . . . arrangement." Iris said the word almost distastefully. "You see, I know he went to Houston to see his attorney. I thought that might be why."

Devon's lips parted in shocked dismay. An attorney. After what had happened last night, he had rushed away to see his attorney. Iris must be right. The entire situation had become too much for him to handle, so he intended to put an end to it by getting rid of her. But he didn't need the aid of an attorney to accomplish that. She could certainly take a hint. Her pride surged forth in rebellion at the thought of him coming back and telling her to leave. If only she could get away before he could return . . .

"I have to find a way to get out of here," she thought aloud.

Iris exhibited rare perception by grasping her meaning immediately. "But he won't let you take Jonathan," she announced ominously. "You know he won't."

"Well, he'll have to, won't he, if he wants to get rid of me?" Devon countered impatiently. "If I go, Jonathan goes with me."

"He'll take you to court and fight you for him."

"Let him. He won't win."

"Can you be so sure of that?" Sighing dramatically, Iris waved a fluttery, uncertain hand. "Look. There *is* one way you could avoid all that trouble, you know. I mean, now

172

don't get upset at what I'm going to suggest, but . . . but . . . well, Ryan and I could make a good home for Jonathan," she blurted out, eyeing Devon hopefully. "We really could. We both love that baby so much, and, actually, it would probably be best for you if you gave Jonathan to us. I mean, you're so young—you could make a nice life for yourself if you're on your own without a child to tie you down. You do see what I mean, don't you?"

For a moment Devon was too astounded to do more than splutter, but at last her words found a voice. "You are *incredible,* Iris! You really think I might just turn my baby over to you? You must be out of your mind! Jonathan is *my* son! Not yours! You can't have everything! And you'll never have my child, I assure you." Clenching her fists at her sides, she slipped off the bed to glare down at the older girl. "Now get out of my room."

Iris rose slowly to her feet, a flush darkening her cheeks beneath her tan. "I didn't mean to upset you," she said innocently. "It's just that Ryan loves Jonathan so much. You must know that. Why else would he have flown to Boston the minute he heard you'd had him?"

The blood drained from Devon's cheeks with frightening speed. *"What?"* she gasped weakly. "Are you saying Ryan knew about Jonathan *before* he went to Boston?"

Iris tilted her head to one side bewilderedly. "Well, yes, of course. The private detective he'd hired to find you told him about Jonathan."

A sudden unbidden memory exploded in Devon's mind. Ryan had said their meeting in the Boston restaurant had been no accident, but she hadn't believed him. Nor could she force herself to believe what Iris was saying now. "But that just doesn't make any sense! Why would he have hired someone to find me? He didn't care at all about me."

"Ryan's more decent than you realize," Iris explained, idly fluffing her thick chestnut hair. "He started worrying about you. You know, he realized he had been your first lover, and since first affairs can be very traumatic for some

173

girls, he just wanted to make sure you were okay. Then, of course, he learned about the baby and . . ."

He had decided he wanted his son. And since bringing her to Texas would enable him to exert more influence in a custody battle, he had forced her to come. Sinking down on the edge of the bed, Devon shook her head, unable to believe his cruelty. Then raw resentment stiffened her spine. Green eyes flashing warning, she glared up at Iris.

"Get out," she commanded, her voice deceptively soft. "Get out right now and don't come back."

"But . . ."

"*Go.*"

Iris went, but hesitated at the door. "Honestly, I really didn't mean to upset you. But just think about it all carefully, please. Ryan and I would love Jonathan to—"

"Get out," Devon repeated through clenched teeth, an incongruously menacing expression hardening her delicate features. "Go or I'll throw you out."

Iris hastily closed the door with a startled gasp. Devon's breath expelled in a shuddering sigh. Delayed reaction was making her entire body tremble violently. She turned to reach for the sleeping tablet automatically. Her hand halted in midair when she noticed the pack of cigarettes and matches Iris had left on the bedside table. There in front of her were the two substances Ryan had forbidden her to use, sedatives and tobacco. Smiling grimly, she scooped up the blue pill and tossed it into her mouth, washing it down with a swallow of water from the glass on the table. Then trembling fingers took a cigarette from the pack. Holding it awkwardly between her lips, she struck a match to light it. She inhaled, coughed violently, then inhaled again, something perverse driving her on. So he thought he could tell her what do! Well, he was wrong! To hell with his majesty and his royal commands. After the way he had hurt her, he dared to try to take Jonathan away from her, too! Knowing that, Devon was not in any mood to let Ryan control her life a moment longer.

* * *

At first, Devon thought it was a nightmare. Something was grabbing her up and carrying her swiftly away. Then, struggling to overcome her sleepiness, she realized with terror that the arms around her were very real. Her eyes flew open. She stifled a scream when she recognized Luke Bishop's face. Instinct made her push at his chest. "What are you doing?" she cried. "Where are you taking me?"

"Be still," he muttered grimly. "It's a fire."

"Jonathan!" she nearly screamed, the horror of the word overwhelming her as she fought to escape Luke's arms. "I have to get Jonathan!"

"He's safe outside," Luke muttered, tightening his hold on her. "Miss Jenkins got him out."

Devon's entire body went limp with the relief that washed over her and her head fell against Luke's shoulder. He deposited her safely by the split-rail fence where Iris and Maggie stood, then ran back to the house. Questions started crowding Devon's mind.

"Where's the fire? How did it start?" she asked Maggie, taking her sleeping son from the older woman's arms. "Is it a bad one?"

Iris nudged Maggie's arm, then the two of them exchanged glances. Turning back, Maggie coughed nervously as she touched Devon's arm. As she opened her mouth to speak, Iris beat her to it.

"I tried to wake you, really I did," she said shrilly, wringing her hands. "I woke up and smelled the smoke, and I went in to get Jonathan when I saw the smoke was coming from . . . from *your* room. I just . . ."

"My room?" Devon exclaimed disbelievingly. "The smoke couldn't have been coming from my room! I would have known if there was a fire in there."

For an odd, fleeting instant Iris seemed almost to smile. Then she hesitated, as if reluctant to say more. She quickly overcame that reluctance, however. "You were sleeping so soundly, Devon; that's why you didn't know about the fire. After I took Jonathan to Maggie, I went back to wake you, but I shook you and shook you and you just wouldn't wake up. It was getting so smoky. I got scared and ran for Luke. Oh, thank God he got you out! I felt so awful about having to leave you."

Devon felt awful, too, though not for the same reason. As she stared at the two women, her face went almost gray. There had been a fire in her room, but even the smell of smoke hadn't roused her. She had slept through it all while Iris had been the one to remove Jonathan from danger. It was the sleeping pill, she thought with a tortured moan. She had risked her son's life for the sake of a full night's sleep. *Unforgivable.* Pulling the thin blanket away from Jonathan's face, she touched his cheek with trembling fingers. Her irresponsibility might have killed him. That made her an unfit mother, didn't it? Of course, it did. How much more unfit could a mother be?

"Oh, God, I can't believe I didn't wake up," she whispered, her mouth crumpling with self-recrimination. "A fire and I didn't even wake up!"

"You've been ill, dear," Maggie said, placing a comforting arm around her shoulders. "That's why you didn't wake up; I'm sure of it. So you can't blame yourself."

But Devon did, especially when Luke appeared a few minutes later.

"Wasn't much of a fire," he commented laconically, stroking the bridge of his nose with one finger. "Not much damage done at all. Cigarette dropped in the trash basket, looks like."

Turning away, clutching Jonathan to her, Devon groaned inwardly. A cigarette! She had smoked two from the pack Iris had left! Now she had to face the guilt of knowing she had started the fire as well as sleeping through it! But she wasn't at all sure she *could* face it.

All through the rest of the night and into the next day, Devon berated herself constantly. So her emotions had taken a terrific beating in the past weeks—that was no excuse for what had happened. And she could never, ever let it happen again! Jonathan was just a helpless baby. She had to concern herself exclusively with taking care of him, even if her personal life was a shambles.

Overwrought with guilt, she couldn't sit still. Every few minutes, she hurried from her room to the nursery to make sure Jonathan was all right. It was silly, she knew, to run back and forth to check on him, but it was reassuring to find him napping peacefully in his crib each time.

Back in her own room, all the questions would start nagging at her again. How had she slept through it all, the smoke and Iris trying to shake her awake? Those sleeping pills had never seemed very powerful before, only mildly relaxing. Yet she had been so very tired last night. On the other hand, she could almost remember grinding out both cigarettes in the brass ash tray on the bedside table. With a puzzled frown, she suddenly recalled that fleeting smile Iris had quickly hidden last night. Why had she smiled like that? Unless . . . no! Devon shook her head in disbelief. Iris couldn't possibly have started the fire! Could she? If she had, why?

None of the questions were answerable, but they bombarded her brain relentlessly until she was emotionally exhausted. Was she trying to place the blame on Iris to absolve herself of feelings of guilt? She just didn't know. A jumble of confusing suspicions plagued her.

It didn't help at all when she nearly stumbled across Iris in the hall as she started on another pilgrimage to Jonathan's room. The older girl's eyes flicked over her almost accusingly. "I just came to tell you I'm going home for the night," Iris explained, examining one slightly uneven fingernail. "Mother is having very important guests for dinner and she insists I be there. Besides, Ryan comes back tomorrow, and, frankly, I'd rather not be here when he hears about last night. I get so upset when he loses his temper."

Devon didn't answer. Clasping her arms together behind her back, she stood her ground, staring back at Iris. Suddenly the older girl moved closer, then looked up and down the hall. "You still want to leave here, don't you?" she whispered. "I could help you get away before Ryan comes back, you know."

Devon frowned suspiciously. "Why would you be willing to do that? Wouldn't Ryan be furious with you if you helped Jonathan and me leave?"

"No, not Jonathan too, you fool!" Iris snapped, raising her voice slightly. "Just you, of course. If you took the baby, Ryan would just go after you."

"Are you saying you expect me to leave without Jonathan?" Devon asked incredulously. "Didn't you hear a word I said last night? I'm not giving you my baby! Where I go, he goes."

A vindictive sneer curled Iris's lips. "You can still say that after you almost set the whole house on fire?" she questioned sarcastically. "You still think you have the right to keep that baby after nearly letting him burn to death?"

Devon bristled, unwilling to listen to such abusive accusations, especially from the person who might have started the fire. Drawing herself up to her full height, she challenged Iris. "I think you should know I suspect *you* started that fire, and I plan to tell Ryan about my suspicions."

"So? He'll never believe you. Do you really expect him to ever trust you?" Iris countered viciously. "Or a court? Oh, no, nobody will be able to trust you if I tell about the sleeping pill I saw on the table last night. You took it and were so knocked out that I couldn't even shake you awake. Oh, if I told that, Ryan would win custody of Jonathan just like that!" She snapped her fingers.

Devon stared at the girl who had turned into a Mr. Hyde before her eyes. Where was the gentle, none-too-bright Iris? Had she been concealing this vicious alter ego all these weeks? Though she had decided Iris was sneaky and two-faced, Devon hadn't expected such irrefutable proof. Momentarily stunned by the sudden transformation, she soon regained her composure. "Many people take sleeping pills, and I don't think it's considered a crime. So Ryan won't get Jonathan away from me just because I took *one*."

Iris laughed nastily. "Dream on, honey. I could make you sound like a real drug addict."

"You could try," Devon amended, maintaining an outward calm, though she was trembling inside. "You'd have to prove it, though, and you couldn't."

"Money can buy proof of anything, and don't you forget it!" Iris exclaimed. "So you might as well pack up and be prepared to go *without Jonathan*. I'll come back in the morning to pick you up. Then our foreman will fly you to Corpus Christi. That will end this stupid mess once and for all. Ryan will have his son, and we can start a life finally. And you'll get by too, I'm sure of it. You can always find another rich old man to marry. Or maybe you can write a bestseller."

Thoroughly disgusted, Devon turned away. She opened the nursery door and stepped inside. Hesitating a second, she glanced back over her shoulder to say softly, "Don't come back tomorrow on my account. I won't be going anywhere with you." After closing the door on Iris's explicit curse, she leaned heavily against it, still clutching the knob. She was afraid to imagine what Ryan *would* say and do when he heard about last night. He would automatically blame her for the fire. She knew it. It would be useless to tell him what she suspected. Iris was right—he would never believe that, never in a million years.

CHAPTER ELEVEN

Late that night, Devon lay in bed, staring up at the shadows dancing on the ceiling. With all the self-restraint she could muster, she was trying not to panic at the thought of what the next few months could bring. Last night she had handed Ryan a very effective weapon to use against her in a custody battle. But since she couldn't erase what had happened, she had to look to the future. For Jonathan's sake, she would have to be strong, even if Iris did follow through with her threats.

Devon smiled ruefully in the darkness. What a surprise Iris had turned out to be, sort of a wolf in sheep's clothing. Now Devon had to suspect all those indiscreet remarks Iris had made had not been indiscreet at all, but deliberate attempts to wound. And Iris's behavior last evening justified Devon's wondering if maybe she had deliberately lost her during their ride together. Devon was virtually certain Iris had deliberately set the fire in her room. It wasn't particularly pleasant to know she was hated with such vicious intensity, yet it was better to have some understanding of an enemy.

Besides, Iris didn't really matter all that much. It was Ryan's potentially hurtful actions that Devon knew she must steel herself against. Though she had tried not to, she still loved him, and he could cause her great pain so easily. He did it every day simply by not loving her in return.

Devon ran trembling fingers through her hair, then tensed when she heard heavy footfalls in the hall. Her door swung open suddenly and the tall, broad silhouette of a man filled her doorway.

"Devon?" Ryan said softly, his melodious voice unmistakable.

"Ryan?" she responded bewilderedly, not certain if she should be relieved or dismayed.

He came in, closing the door quietly behind him. He strode across the room and sat down on the edge of the bed beside her. Laying a strangely possessive hand on her abdomen, he reached out with the other to switch on the lamp, illuminating the room in a soft, warm glow.

Devon blinked up at him, her body still tensed. At her questioning murmur, he smiled and touched gentle fingertips to her lips. "Just listen a minute," he commanded, his voice low. "Maggie heard what Iris was saying to you this afternoon and she got suspicious. She called me home, and I've just been talking to Luke. He says the fire in the trash basket couldn't possibly have been burning as long as Iris claimed—there wasn't enough smoke or ashes. He says too that you awoke almost the moment he picked you up, so he doesn't believe Iris ever tried to awaken you. His theory is that she took Jonathan to Maggie, *then* came in here to toss a lighted cigarette in the trash basket. After she saw that some of the papers had caught fire, she ran to him, saying she couldn't get you up. And after what Maggie heard her saying to you today, I think his theory's right. So you have no reason to blame yourself for what happened last night. I wanted you to know that before I said anything else."

Devon's first reaction was one of overwhelming relief. She really *hadn't* been responsible for the fire. And now even Ryan understood that Iris was the only other logical suspect. Hoping she wasn't just dreaming, Devon sat up in bed, brushing a tendril of hair back from her face. "I thought she might have done it," she admitted faintly. "But I really don't understand why she'd do something so . . . so *horrid.*"

181

Ryan shook his head. "She apparently wanted you to leave Jonathan, according to what Maggie heard. So I can only guess that she miscalculated and assumed I'd let you leave here if you didn't take him with you."

"And I thought she was simple-minded," Devon whispered with an amazed, resigned smile. "Such a complicated plot just to get rid of me. She must want to marry you very badly."

Ryan's jaw tightened as he muttered angrily, "I don't know if that was her motive or not, and I really don't give a damn. All I know is that if she were here right now, I think I'd . . ." He broke off, cupping Devon's face in his hands. "I'm just sorry that she hurt you. What she did last night was unforgivable."

"I . . . I guess she just loves you," Devon whispered, averting her eyes. "And she hates me for causing you to delay your marriage. I can understand that. You will too, Ryan; you'll forgive her. You're just angry now."

"Devon, look at me," he coaxed softly, his thumbs lifting her chin. "I don't know exactly what kind of lies Iris has been telling you the past few weeks, but I never planned to marry her. Supposedly, she was trying to convince you of that all this time. She was telling *me* that you didn't care whether I married her or not, that all you cared about was getting away from this place and me." He paused, his darkening gaze searching Devon's face. "Don't you think I would have married her years before I even met you if she was the woman I wanted? I could have; she'd like to live on one of the largest ranches in Texas, which is what we'd own together if we married. But *I* never wanted that or her, Dev. Our engagement was strictly for my father's benefit. It meant nothing to me, and she knew that because I told her so."

"But the Dallas newspaper! In the society column Iris was called your fiancée."

"Speculation, or maybe Iris planted the story herself. God, I don't know," he muttered, sliding his fingers into

182

Devon's thick, silky hair. "But however it got into the paper, it wasn't true. "You, Dev, *you* are the only woman I've ever wanted to spend my life with."

Though Devon's heart began to beat jerkily, she was too afraid to allow herself to believe him. She shook her head. "But Iris . . . said you only came back to Boston because you knew about Jonathan and wanted to take him away from me since she can't have children."

"Good God! I just told you she's obviously been filling your head full of lies, so how can you believe that?" Ryan asked rather impatiently. "If she can't have children, then it's news to me. And I assure you I went to Boston to see *you.* I had no idea Jonathan even existed. I did know about your marriage to Andrews, of course. That's why I didn't go back there earlier. When you never answered my letters or returned my calls in two months, I was going crazy with worry. So I hired a man to find you. But when he reported back that you were married, I tried to forget you. Without any success at all, I might add. Finally I decided I had to see you again, even though you were married. So I flew back, discovered where you worked, and followed you to that restaurant."

"How can I believe that, Ryan?" she protested weakly. "There were never any letters to answer or calls to return." Her lips trembled as common sense warred with a need to believe him. At last, she shook her head. "No letters. Not one. I waited and waited, but . . ."

"I wrote you, Devon," he insisted, spanning her trim waist with caressing hands. "I can't prove I wrote, but I *can* prove I called. With my father in the hospital in Houston, I stayed in a hotel. They keep records of long-distance calls. I can get you the proof, or . . ." His hands on her tightened. "Or you can trust me. You can concede that Andrews could have taken the letters. It would have been easy. Remember? All of you shared that one mailbox."

That was true. It had been an old house converted to

183

apartments and no one objected to sharing a common mailbox. And the phone . . . She hadn't had one in her apartment because there had been a convenient pay phone in the hall. Anybody could have answered when Ryan called. If he called . . . But he said he could prove he had. Yet . . . she gazed up at him, tortured by confusion. "But why would Ben have stolen your letters? Why wouldn't he have told me you called? And came! He didn't like you much and thought we were totally unsuited for each other, but still . . ."

"Maybe . . . oh, God, I don't know *why* he did it. All I'm sure of is that he did. It's the only reasonable explanation," Ryan exclaimed bitterly. "Maybe he thought he was protecting you from me or something."

Ryan's theory triggered a sudden, shattering memory. Devon gasped, gripping his arms. "Oh, Lord, he said something to me before he died! It didn't make any sense at all then, but now . . . He said something like, 'I did it for you. Remember that. You're too much like my Emily to be involved with someone like Wilder. I did it for your own good.' " Devon shook her head, still bewildered. Although she was beginning to understand that Ben had deceived her and that Ryan really had written and called, had even gone to Boston as he claimed, she had been hurt too much in the past year to give up all her defenses now. And too many unanswered questions swirled in her mind.

"But you . . . you've let Iris stay here so often since I came. Why, when you must have known she was upsetting me?" Devon questioned him urgently. "You *must* care something about her or you wouldn't have wanted her here with you all the time."

"But she wasn't here to be with *me*," he explained wearily. "Iris has always been close to Maggie and was here as her guest, not mine. Of course, neither Maggie nor I knew how she'd been treating you until this morning."

"But you always took her side against me," Devon persisted rather petulantly. "You told me that instead of

184

writing, I should try to be more like her. And even when
. . . when I got lost, you blamed me completely."

"Devon, you silly, I didn't mean it when I said you
should be more like her. I just resented your writing because I thought your career meant much more to you than
I did. I thought you'd married Andrews for that same
reason, to further your career through the help his friends
could give you." Ryan shook his head. "All right, I admit
I was wrong not to suspect Iris of deliberately losing you
that day you two went riding. But I never said I didn't
blame her somewhat. I very nearly killed her when she
rode back here that day without you. And I think I would
have killed her if something terrible had happened to you
out there. Right now, knowing she probably did lose you
on purpose, I could . . ."

Though he didn't finish, Devon recognized the sincerity
in his protectively angry tone. Suddenly she could fight
him no longer. With a muffled sob, she propelled herself
into arms that enfolded her with rough urgency. "Does
that mean you really care about me?" she murmured tearfully against his shoulder. "Does it, Ryan?"

"*Care!* God, yes, I care. I love you. I never stopped!"
He groaned, entangling long, lean fingers in her thick hair,
pulling her head back, seeking and finding her mouth. As
his firm lips parted the tender sweetness of hers, he gathered her closer, encircling her in strong arms. Curiously
unsteady hands drifted over her, firm and warm though
the thin satiny fabric of her gown, evoking a tremor of
sensual excitement in her as his mouth moved seductively
on hers. His tongue, intimately seeking, tasted hers. Then
his teeth closed gently again and again on her soft lower
lip, as if he hungered insatiably for her.

Devon uttered a soft little cry, nearly a whimper, as his
hand found her breasts, caressing her with gently possessive fingers. "I've dreamed of making love to you nearly
every night the past year," he whispered hoarsely. "But
every time I did, I only woke up frustrated because I was

185

never able to possess you totally, even in a damned dream."

"I had those dreams, too," she breathed. "So many times. Oh, Ryan, I've been so lonely. It's been awful."

"Then I take it you *do* need me? Just a little?"

"Much more than a little," she admitted, no longer able to hold back the tears that had been suppressed far too long.

Murmuring comforting words into her ear, Ryan rocked her in his arms as if she were a child. "Now you cry," he teased. "Devon, if you'd done this weeks ago, we could have talked all this out then and avoided torturing each other."

"I . . . was too proud to cry in front of you."

"Yes, we've both been too proud. Too stupidly proud." With infinite gentleness, he kissed away the tears on her cheeks. Finally, her soft sobs were stilled. Then the warmth of his hands stroking her back began to convey much more than a mere desire to give comfort. They began a slow exploration, his fingertips probing the delicate structure of her spine, downward, ever downward to curve possessively over her rounded hips.

"Ryan, oh, I love you." She sighed, quivering as he caressed her smooth upper thighs, the heel of his hard hand brushing with evocative slowness between them. Her trembling fingers slipped inside his suit coat to unbutton his vest and shirt, seeking his hair-roughened chest, gliding over the muscular contours of his flesh. Delighted by her ability to arouse him, she smiled sensuously when he groaned as she moved her palms over the hard nubs of his nipples.

"You're trembling," he whispered against her tousled, scented hair. "Trembling as much as you did that first time we made love. Andrews never touched you, did he, Devon?"

She shook her head. "We just needed each other. He was hopelessly ill and I . . . I was pregnant and feeling sick so often that I'd resigned from my job. That's why I married him. It wasn't because I wanted to use him. He was just lonely and so was I. We looked after each other, that's all. He never made love to me. No one except you ever has."

"God, I'm glad!" he muttered roughly. "I couldn't bear the thought of any other man possessing you. You're mine, all mine. No one else can have you."

At his impassioned tone, Devon leaned back against the arm that supported her, green eyes dark with renewed confusion. "The other night then, why didn't you . . . why did you stop, Ryan?" she asked hesitantly, appealing color tinting her cheeks. "Why didn't you want me?"

"Not want you!" He groaned, his eyes glittering hotly. "You little idiot, I wanted you like hell."

"Then why . . ."

"Dev, Dr. Turner told me you really shouldn't have another baby for a while, and I promised myself I wouldn't risk getting you pregnant," he explained tenderly. "God knows I've despised myself for what happened that night in Corpus Christi, but, even so, letting you go the other night was the hardest thing I've ever had to do."

Devon moaned softly. "And I thought you'd promised Iris you'd never make love to me again. I thought . . ."

"You thought too many things you shouldn't have," he chided, beginning to press near-bruising kisses down her neck. When her mouth eagerly sought his, he lowered her down onto the mattress, pulling off her scanty gown, devouring her lips, imprisoning her beneath the hardening length of his body. "You're beautiful," he said huskily, lowering his dark head to close his mouth around the invitingly erect tip of one throbbing breast, then the other. His lips took possession, exerting a moist, pulling pressure on the sensitized crests.

An empty ache quickened within her. Her hands urgently slid his coat, shirt, and vest off his shoulders, then moved down to brush across the buckle of his belt.

"Dev, be careful," he warned hoarsely, propping himself up on one elbow to gaze down at her. "It's way past time for us to get married. Maybe we should wait until we are, until we can take the proper precautions. If I make you pregnant now . . ."

"Then you can take care of me and that will make the nine months altogether different," she whispered provocatively. "But you don't have to worry because I'm sure I'll be fine." When she reached up with one finger to trace the firmly shaped outline of his mouth, he suddenly caught her fingertip between his teeth, and she shivered with intensifying desire. She urged him closer again. "I need you so much, Ryan. This time you *have* to make love to me. I can't wait any longer."

His self-control snapped. Arching her to him, he groaned against her parted lips. "I need you, too, Dev, but I'll try to be gentle. I want to be. We've had so little time together that it almost seems as if I've never made love to you. You seem as completely innocent as you did that first time."

"But I'm not," she reminded him swiftly, the tip of her tongue touching one corner of his sensuously carved mouth. "I remember exactly how you can make me feel, and I need for you to make me feel that way again. I want that so much, Ryan."

"And I want you." Passion was tempered with loving gentleness as he slipped her nightgown down her legs, then off completely. When she quivered, his teeth nibbled the rounded curve of one creamy, scented shoulder.

Through lowered lashes, Devon watched as he suddenly stood to strip off his remaining clothes. He came back beside her, his body warm and smooth and taut with latent power. Sun-bronzed questing fingers lingered on the ivory satin fullness of her breasts, then feathered down across her flat abdomen. She trembled and ached with longing so

188

intense she could scarcely breathe. His hand slipped between her thighs, his fingers brushing irresistible warmth, trailing fire over every inch of sensitized skin.

"Touch me, Dev," he commanded, drawing her hand downward.

Finally secure in the certainty of his love, she obeyed, exploring his body for the first time, delighting in the response of aroused masculinity her intimate touch elicited. With a muffled groan, Ryan bore her slight body down into the softness of the mattress. Whispered endearments caressed her lips. His kisses became lingering and possessive, tantalizing preludes to the complete satisfaction they both sought.

Devon's body weakened to warm fluidity. "Ryan, please." She sighed as his firm mouth ravished hers. Her nails pressed into his muscular shoulders. "Please, hurry. Love me."

"Yes, I'm going to. Now," he whispered, his eyes of aqua fire holding her drowsy gaze as his knee gently parted her thighs and her slender, shapely legs entangled with his. A soft, contented sigh of total surrender escaped her. Possessive triumph flared in the dark depths of his eyes. And she was mesmerized, unable to give in to her sudden shyness to look away as his body merged slowly with hers, filling her completely, invading her secret, innermost feminine warmth. Ryan's lips captured her breathless moan of delight, and tears of sheer joy caught in Devon's lower lashes as they came together, mutual love and spellbinding pleasure combining in a new peak of rapture and unity, a new and lasting beginning.

"Dev, love," he murmured, smiling down at the loving luminosity that softened her eyes to deep pools of emerald. "Now, you're really mine again."

"I always was," she answered adoringly. Her breath caught in anticipation of pleasures to come as his mouth possessed hers again. He began to move with rousing slowness until she was upswept in tumultuous passion, feverishly breathing his name against hard lips no longer capable of gentleness.

Holding tight rein on his own desire, Ryan made love to her slowly and with infinite patience, only content when he had taken her to shattering heights of ecstasy. Devon clung to him, crying out faintly as piercing delight rippled in hot, pulsating waves inside her. The waves receded, then unexpectedly crested again with even more throbbing intensity, spreading warmth and indescribable pleasure deep within. Her tremulous cry of fulfillment was muffled against his throat. Her ragged breathing began to slow. Utterly pliant, she wrapped herself closer to him, compelling him to take from her as much ecstasy as he had given.

Day was breaking, filling the room with the soft gray light of dawn. Devon slowly opened her eyes. A slight contented smile curved her lips and she moved her legs lazily, turning her head on the pillow to meet Ryan's warm, loving gaze. He lifted himself up to rest on one elbow and looked down at her. When she closed her teeth gently on the tip of the lean finger he touched to her lips, he smiled wickedly. "Watch yourself, Dev. You might get more of a response than you bargained for."

Smiling back, she whispered primly, "Surely such thoughts aren't proper so early in the morning?"

"And why not? We made love early in the morning after the first night you spent with me. Remember?"

"I remember every single moment we've ever spent together. I just wish there'd been more of them."

"Yes, a whole year wasted," he muttered roughly, trailing feathering fingertips over her cheek. "We have a lot to make up for."

"Umm, that does sound like fun." He rewarded her bold words with a rousing kiss. Laughing softly, she stretched lazily and draped her arms around his neck. "I wonder if Maggie will approve of us getting married," she mused. "She doesn't seem to think I'm suited for life here. She thinks I'm too fragile to be a rancher's wife."

Ryan laughed softly. "But Maggie just doesn't know what a little hellcat you can be, does she?"

"You do, though," Devon replied, regret shadowing her eyes. "Oh, Ryan, I'm sorry I've been so stubborn and so difficult. I'll change, I promise."

"Don't you dare," he commanded, moving swiftly to cover her slender body with his. "I happen to like you just the way you are. There are times when a man wants his woman to have a lot of spirit."

"Oh? And what times do you mean?"

A soft laugh rumbled from deep in Ryan's throat as his dark, narrowing gaze swept over her. "Ah, Dev, if you're still that innocent, I guess maybe I'd better show you what I mean."

"I guess maybe you'd better," she agreed. She slid her arms up around his neck and gave herself up totally to the worshiping wonder of his demanding kiss.

LOOK FOR NEXT MONTH'S
CANDLELIGHT ECSTASY ROMANCES™